first daughter

first
daughter

by Christa Roberts

Story by Jessica Bendinger and Jerry O'Connell
Screenplay by Jessica Bendinger
and Kate Kondell

Bantam Books
new york • toronto • london • sydney • auckland

AGES 10 AND UP

FIRST DAUGHTER
A Bantam Book/August 2004

ISBN: 0-553-49442-2

Visit us on the Web! www.randomhouse.com/teens
Educators and librarians, for a variety of teaching tools,
visit us at www.randomhouse.com/teachers

Published simultaneously in the United States and Canada

Bantam Books is an imprint of Random House Children's Books, a division of Random House, Inc. BANTAM BOOKS and the rooster colophon are registered trademarks of Ran-dom House, Inc.

PRINTED IN THE UNITED STATES OF AMERICA

10   9   8   7   6   5   4   3   2   1

For Olivia,
the shining star of daughters . . .
and William,
my little golden sun

Redmond University
College Admission Essay

What's So Special About My Life?
By Samantha Mackenzie

Once upon a time, there was a little girl who was just like every other girl. And that girl would be, well, me. Sam. Samantha if my mother is in earshot. I've participated in more extra-curricular activities than even I can remember. My favorites have always been girl-oriented . . . but with a special twist.

Example #1: I love ballet. Watching it, doing it, wearing old leather toe slippers around in my bedroom. But I don't have to dance across a stage to express what I'm feeling. Did you know that some of the best ballet moves can be done in the privacy of your own swimming pool? Did you know that cannonballs are really stretching the same muscles as pliés? Scout's honor, it's true. You should try it sometime.

Example #2: I love to host tea parties. The whole nine yards—the fancy china, the little cucumber and cream cheese sandwiches with the crusts trimmed off, Ascot-inspired hats with gigantic flowers and ribbons. But if a party crasher invaded the party—say, a toad with a heavy-duty ribbit—I'd just as soon slosh the tea out of the cup and trap him as a perfect specimen of nature to study (I'm not too big on proper etiquette). And moreover, I'm not at all afraid of bugs or reptiles or rodents. Not even mice! In fact, I kind of like them.

Example #3: Well, I could go on, but this essay would get way too unwieldy.

I have had a problem, though, a problem that has plagued me since I was a little girl. You know how when you get braces or a pimple or a heinous haircut (that would be the shag for me—it was so not "back," as my hairstylist tried to persuade me), and you are convinced that the whole world is staring at you, secretly laughing behind your back and cracking jokes just out of earshot? Well for me, the whole world really is watching. (But I digress. More on that later)

But, eventually, like the rest of my peers, I muddled through, and as I blossomed, I became more comfortable in my own skin. Like any normal teenager, I enjoy going to parties, though the crowd I run with is admittedly a bit stuffier than that of most people (but, as my mom's chief of staff is always telling me, I must be diplomatic when it comes to diplomats), and, oh, lots of other normal things, like ordering pizza and surfing the Net and doing volunteer work and playing cards.

I still haven't quite gotten over the feeling that every move I make is being scrutinized (though I have stopped reading all the gossip papers. Ugh! Who needs them?) But as I've grown older, I've been able to look outside myself, and appreciate the wisdom of my elders. (And believe me when I say, despite all the wonderful things I have learned, I am elder-ed out. I love old people, but come on! I need to be with people my own age. People like the freshman class at Redmond University. ☺

In short, I want you to know that my life isn't any more special than that of any of the other applicants who are hoping to attend Redmond University in the fall. I grew up happy, with the love of a mother and father who idolized me, and who were the center of my world in an old white house in Washington, D.C., that, for us, is just plain old home.

And that's how I would like to be treated. Just like plain old me. Sam MacKenzie.

With best regards,
Samantha MacKenzie
First Daughter

(I'm sorry, but my mom's personal secretary insists I sign all of my correspondence this way, and if she happens to read this I want to make sure I did it properly so she doesn't withhold sending it off to you. But for the record, I really am just plain old Sam. Thank you.)

chapter**one**

As the elevator doors whooshed open, Samantha Mackenzie took one last semi-private breath. Her designer ball gown was expertly fitted; her straight long brown hair was pulled back into a tight, sleek chignon; diamond studs sparkled on her earlobes; and a delicate gold chain was clasped at the nape of her neck.

She looked like any other teenager headed to her senior prom.

"Lucky Charm in two," Secret Service Agent Bock said from behind her, speaking her official code name into his wristpiece.

The prom . . . I wish! Samantha thought wistfully as she traipsed down the plushly carpeted hallway toward the White House ballroom, her new high heels pressing uncomfortably against her pedicured toes. She glanced over at the four Secret Service agents who surrounded her as she walked, their faces as familiar to her as her own. On second thought, maybe it was a blessing in disguise that she hadn't been allowed to attend her school's senior dance.

I would have spent the entire night dancing with my security detail. How fun.

Tonight was a big night, but for a different reason. Tonight was Samantha's last official White House function before she left for college in the morning. But instead of spending the night reminiscing with her high school buddies—not that she had any—she was representing the United States at the latest White House ball.

Inside the grand ballroom, the evening's festivities were in full swing. Men in tuxedos and svelte women in pricey ball gowns stood sipping cocktails under twinkling glass chandeliers. White-jacketed servers proffered trays of chilled shrimp and chicken satay to the elite invited guests.

As usual, Senator Cronin is cutting a rug, Sam thought, suppressing a smile as she spotted the portly Midwest politician with two left feet twirling by with the French ambassador's unsuspecting wife. Sam's parents stood greeting their guests in the traditional receiving line that was set up alongside the ballroom's main entrance, her mother in an elegant silk dress with upswept hair and classic jewelry, her father strong and impressive in his American-designed tuxedo.

Catching her mother's beckoning eye, Samantha hurried to take her place in line beside them. Sometimes she wondered what would happen if she called out, "In a minute, Ma. I want to drink a soda at the bar first." Or, "Do you want me to grab you a plate of cheese and crackers?"

Not that she would ever dare do that. That kind of behavior wouldn't exactly go over well.

As she had done hundreds of times

before, Samantha put on her camera-ready smile and began to greet the foreign dignitaries who were filing into the ballroom. "It's a pleasure to meet you," she said politely to a man she vaguely recognized from a *Time* cover story. "Delightful to see you again," she said to the prime minister of Canada with a cordial handshake.

Tonight, though, Samantha's heart wasn't in the standard meet-and-greet. Just once, she wished she could spend a Saturday evening doing something normal, like going to a movie and grabbing a pepperoni pizza afterward. Or bowling. Or hanging out at the mall. *Or . . . or going to some wild keg party and checking out cute boys*, she thought, wincing as the German ambassador gave her hand a tight squeeze.

"Why, if it isn't little Samantha. How you have *grown!*" gushed the next guest in line, the wife of a South American diplomat. "I remember when you were running through the halls of the Governor's Mansion clad in just your diapers!"

Samantha managed to beam back. *Anything but this.*

"Something's wrong with Sam," she heard her mother say under her breath to her father a few minutes later. After years in the public eye, Samantha had become a pro at reading lips *and* making out words barely above a decibel.

"Impossible," her father answered through a toothy smile. "It's an election year, remember?"

Her mother shook her head. "She could use some downtime."

"And starting November fifth, she can have all the downtime she needs."

November fifth. November fifth. It seemed like an eternity until the presidential election would actually be over with. There had been so much discussion about it, Sam felt as if the date were permanently tattooed on her brain.

As the band struck up a new tune, Samantha's father left his place in line. "Feel like a dance with your old man?" he asked her, his eyes twinkling.

Samantha smiled back, reaching to take his hand.

She had had more than enough fancy White House functions to last a lifetime.

But she always had room on her dance card for her dad. Who just happened to be the President of the United States.

"Press conference at nine. Marine One at nine-fifteen to Air Force One at ten." Liz Pappas, the extremely efficient White House press secretary, took a minute to glance down at her omnipresent clipboard. *Why does she even bother to look at that?* Samantha wondered, gazing at her reflection in her bedroom mirror. She sighed and took a few more bobby pins out of her hair. *If I know Liz, she probably has the whole schedule memorized anyway.*

Liz went on. "Travel from ten to—"

"Hold that thought, Liz," Samantha said, cutting her off. Hearing the point-by-point details of how her departure for Redmond University was to be handled was way too overwhelming. "Let's pretend that tomorrow I'm heading off to college. I grab my bags—which I packed myself—throw them in my adorable vintage Volkswagen Beetle, next to my cooler that has a beer hiding under the bologna sandwiches." She closed her eyes, imagining the whole fantasy coming true. "My parents cry—their only child is growing up, and so forth. And then I do it. I drive off—like the normal, run-of-the-mill kid I am." She turned to face Liz.

For a moment, Liz's all-business demeanor softened. In her heart, Samantha knew that Liz Pappas wasn't out to ruin her life. Her minute-by-minute scheduling of Samantha's day wasn't anything personal. She was just doing her job—a job that she happened to be very good at. *She'd send me to a spa in Hawaii on Air Force One if that's what my father's schedule demanded.*

Still, though, it didn't hurt a girl to dream a little.

"Ignorance is bliss," Samantha said, giving Liz a small shrug. "Whaddaya say?"

Liz smiled sympathetically. "I say, sweet dreams, normal, boring girl." She walked to the door, then turned back. "And better move that beer—under the sandwiches is the first place they'll look."

"Duly noted," Samantha said with a resigned smile. "Thanks."

Maybe it did hurt a girl to dream a little, she decided as she removed her watch and placed it on her dresser. It made it that much harder to accept what could never be.

Five steps. Wait seven seconds. Then five more steps. Wait . . . wait . . . wait . . . *Go!* Years of practice had helped Samantha perfect the art of avoiding the video security monitor. Quick as a caffeinated mouse, she scurried into the East Room, down the hallway, and into the nearby elevator, clad in nothing but her pink bathrobe.

When the doors opened, she was in one of her favorite parts of the White House.

The huge, state-of-the-art kitchen.

She walked over to the wall and flipped on some lights, then walked inside the industrial-sized refrigerator. "Hmmm," she said, looking over four freshly made apple pies and a huge container of rice pudding. "What do we have here?" She picked up a gooey chocolate cake and stepped back into the kitchen. "Mmmm," she said, sticking her finger in the frosting and licking it off. This could almost make up for the two hours she had stood in the receiving line.

Taking a quick glance around to make sure no one was there, Samantha scooped more frosting off with her finger.

Then, suddenly, the lights went out.

Shoot! Caught again!

"Did you take the southern route to the stairwell or the northern route through the access hall?"

Samantha's shoulders relaxed. It was her father. "Eastern route, actually. Two elevators, one moving walkway, turn left at the Lincoln arches," she told him. "Lesser-known, but very effective."

Her father chuckled. "Good choice. Eastern's one of my favorites, actually. . . . Lincoln arches is a nice twist, though." He took out a knife from a kitchen drawer and cut himself a piece of cake. "But, you know, if you're going to take the cake, you have to pay the toll."

Samantha leaned up on her tiptoes and gave her father a chocolaty kiss on his left cheek. Immediately he pointed to his other cheek as well.

"Inflation?" she said, in mock protest. "You should really do something about that, Dad."

As she leaned in to comply, her father took her gently by the arms and started to twirl her across the kitchen floor.

"Oh, no, not the dancing," Samantha moaned, keeping her feet in sync with his. Despite her protests, she treasured moments like these—normal, private moments without the press corps barking questions or her father's staff rushing him from one meeting to another.

"Dad?" she said, leaning her head against his chest. A thin ray of moonlight cast a dull glow into the darkened room. "I need to say something."

He stopped humming the tune of the song they had danced to earlier at the ball. "What is it?"

"About tomorrow," she began, her

stomach churning nervously. "I was thinking . . . maybe I *should* go alone. It's hard
enough to blend in having a team of Secret
Service agents to carry my books." She took
a deep breath. "What I'm saying is, I just
want to be like everybody else."

Please, please, please, she silently begged.
*Give me a chance at having a real college experi-
ence.*

Her father smiled down at her, then
kissed her forehead. "Samantha, you're *not*
like everybody else."

Disappointment welled through her
and her feet dragged slowly through the
motions, kicking the refrigerator shut as
they passed. She hadn't really expected him
to go along with her plan.

But it would have been nice.

chapter**two**

Saying goodbye ended up taking a lot longer than Samantha had anticipated. It wasn't just a wave to her parents and the press corps and then off she went.

First she had to make the rounds of the White House one last time and say farewell to the official florists, bid adieu to the French-born chocolatiers, write a perfectly proper note to the calligraphers—and she couldn't forget to do her highly choreographed handshake routine with Sal and Charlie, her two favorite maintenance men, who worked deep in the underground tunnels to which tourist groups never gained access.

"Eu sou selvagem com fome. Onde está meu patron saint do alimento?" Samantha said breezily in fluent Portuguese, her black pumps clicking as she walked through the White House kitchen. "Joam?"

Up from behind a huge stainless steel work island popped Joam Carlos, one of her favorite staff members, a large plastic bag in his hands. The flamboyant Brazilian chef always made her laugh, and he made the best chicken taquitos she had ever tasted.

"Magic candies to make you gorgeous," Joam explained, handing Samantha the bag. He gave a little shrug in his stiff standard white chef's toque. "No brains, no beauty. I'm sorry God dealt you such a bad hand."

"Come with me," Samantha urged, her eyes twinkling. "Why work here when you can shine in a university cafeteria?" A pang hit her as she realized this would be the

19

last time in a long time that she'd dance this silly little tango with her old friend. "I'm really gonna miss you, Joam," she said quietly, her voice no longer playful.

Joam's eyes looked like they were about to flow over with tears. He cleared his throat. "Try not to get straight Fs," he choked out in accented English. "I know it will be hard with such a tiny brain." He leaned forward and gave Samantha a hard hug, then dashed off.

Sam wiped her eyes. She was so excited, but this was so hard.

Liz Pappas materialized at her side, dressed in her customary dark suit. "It's time," she said, giving Samantha a pert nod.

Samantha nodded back. "Let's do it."

They walked briskly down the White House corridor toward the Rose Garden, where the national press was waiting with their klieg lights, cable coils, TV cameras, and probably a bouquet of microphones. Liz rattled off orders and security details the entire way. "They'll ask you about your expectations, your hopes, your major, and you'll say—"

"Just what I'm supposed to," Samantha said dutifully as several other staff members fell in with their entourage. "Don't worry, Liz. I'm set." Then a thought hit her. "Does anyone have my—"

"Got it," Liz said with a smile. The press secretary took Samantha's charm bracelet from her suit coat pocket and fastened it around Sam's wrist as they walked. Sam tried to keep her face relaxed and her pace steady as a makeup person whipped out a puff and began powdering her face.

The old familiar butterflies began fluttering as they entered, then exited an elevator and walked to the eastern staircase, where the First Lady, the First Lady's chief of staff, and a pack of harried-looking assistants came walking quickly toward them from one direction, while the President, his press secretary, his communications director, his assistants, and the usual assortment of Secret Service agents came at them from the other.

"So remember, Samantha, you're just like any other American family," Liz said encouragingly as the three groups converged and headed toward the wide double doors that led to the Rose Garden.

Sam opened her mouth to say something sarcastic, but fell silent. Maybe Liz was right. When she blocked out all the craziness that was a part of her family's life, she knew that deep down, they *were* just like everyone else.

Or at least I want us to be.

Sam's heart went out to her mother as the First Lady took a deep breath, then smoothed down her brown linen pants and adjusted the cream-colored sweater that was tied around her shoulders. *I guess watching your baby leave for college is a pretty difficult thing to do*, Samantha thought as their eyes met. *Especially when you have to do it in front of Peter Jennings.*

Her father was casually dressed in his I'm-a-regular-guy clothes, which for him meant jeans, a blue gingham shirt, and a soft suede jacket. He took her hand and squeezed it. "I love you, Samantha," he whispered, kissing the top of her head.

Her mother took her other hand. "Me too, darling."

And when the double doors opened, the President, the First Lady, and the First Daughter were hand in hand—the picture of domestic perfection.

Samantha's mouth was bone dry. *What I wouldn't give for a bottle of water!* she thought, squinting out at the sea of reporters' faces, each of them hanging on her father's every word. *Really ice-cold water.* Sure, the gathered media were interested in her as well, but Samantha knew that they were really hoping that her father might segue into his Education Reform Initiative, or talk about the Youth Literacy Program— or maybe even discuss his opinion on the Middle East.

But Sam knew he wouldn't. He had told her that today wasn't for giving a stump speech—today was about her, Samantha Mackenzie.

And Sam knew he meant it.

"Mr. President, how do you feel about your only child going to school so far away?" a reporter called out.

The President raised an eyebrow. "I feel we should move the nation's capital to California."

Amid the appreciative chuckles, another reporter asked, "Samantha, will you miss D.C.? Better yet, what will you miss least?"

"That's easy—the press," she deadpanned. Then she gave them a genuine smile. "No offense. It's just that I'm really excited to experience life as a normal kid, having a normal college experience."

And then, after a few more rounds of questions, Samantha was off to board Marine One to do just that.

When they disembarked Air Force One, Samantha was given a list of security precautions that had been put in place on campus. She read over it as the presidential limousine traveled down the main drag of Berkeley toward Redmond University.

Bulletproof glass has been installed in Lucky Charm's dorm room window, as well as in the windows of her classrooms and her cafeteria.

Sam didn't know if she should feel comforted that they were taking such precautions or worried that they had to take such precautions.

All city postal units along the presidential motorcade route have been removed for the day.

Phew! One more day that she was safe from crazies who tossed unfriendly packages into unsuspecting mailboxes.

The Secret Service has conducted thorough examinations of the campus, its grounds, and dorm floors with its canine units and will continue to do so throughout Lucky Charm's tenure.

Okay, there went any hope for blending in with the masses.

All visitors on campus today will enter through metal detectors.

Was she going to college or prison?

Samantha tossed the list on the black leather seat and stared out the window. She always felt really sorry for the poor Secret Service agents who had to run alongside the presidential limousine. Not only did they risk being shot at by some lunatic in the crowd, they had to run at a pretty good clip for several miles.

A squadron of motorcycle policemen led the way, followed by police cars and several black Suburbans with pitch-black windows. Crowds lined the main street in town, and Sam spotted National Guardsmen every few hundred feet. Some people were cheering, some waved signs, and some just stared. And of course there were the inevitable protesters, holding signs that read NO MORE MACKENZIE!

Beside her, the First Lady scribbled some notes on a computer printout.

"This is not what I dreamed of," Samantha said, slumping down in her seat.

"We know, honey," her mother said sympathetically, touching her shoulder. She handed the papers to the President. "Next life."

Then, at last, Samantha recognized the lush green grounds and impressive entry gate of Redmond University's campus. *We're really here*, Samantha thought excitedly, hope welling up inside her. If there was ever a place that she could start fresh, it was here, three thousand miles from home.

More press awaited them, their cameras clicking and video cameras rolling. Military snipers with MP5 rifles were positioned up on the roofs of the dormitories and classroom buildings. Samantha tucked a stray piece of hair behind her ear and adjusted her lightweight jacket as the limousine entered a secure area near a tall ivy-covered brick building she immediately recognized from the college admissions catalog as Woody House, her dorm. To her dismay, she also recognized the uniform of the university's marching band . . . and the hundred or so students who were wearing it filled her with dread.

"Tell me that band is just for show," she

pleaded with her father. His expression told her it wasn't. "Oh, please, God, not 'Hail to the Chief.'"

And right on cue, the band struck up their best rendition of the song Samantha had heard at least once a day for the past four years.

Heaving a resigned sigh, Samantha dabbed a tiny bit of lip gloss on her lips and put her shoes back on. She watched as her mother put on her First Lady face. First, she rubbed her temples in small circles—two back, two forward—and then took one deep breath.

Melanie Mackenzie, aka Mom, had left the building.

The First Lady was back in town.

Samantha waved to the crowd as she and her parents exited the limousine and her father shook hands with the university's dean. They made the usual small talk that people do in front of large gatherings; then her father waved once more to the crowd.

"It's not too late to call Georgetown," he

said to her through his teeth, smiling widely. "You can live at home. Free laundry."

"I didn't choose a school three thousand miles away for nothing," Sam said, her voice light.

A few minutes later, staff began to unload her things, but to her surprise, her father waved them off. "I insist on doing the job myself," he said firmly.

Seeing the President chipping in made a great photo op. *But he never would have done this if he'd realized just how much I'd packed!* Sam thought as he struggled to pull one of her many pieces of luggage from the limousine's trunk.

She had a feeling this was going to take a long, long time.

chapter**three**

"Hi, hi, hello," Samantha said to the awestruck students lining the second floor hallway of Woody House. She tried to look friendly and accessible as she and her parents, luggage in hand, along with two Secret Service agents, followed Liz Pappas to her room.

Two other freshman girls gaped at her. "Ohmigod!" one of them screamed as she frantically punched a number into her cell phone. "My sister won't believe this!"

"She's much taller in person," the other

one muttered, her eyes skimming over Sam.

Oh, no, I don't feel self-conscious at all, Samantha thought as the first girl thrust her cell phone at her. "Here! Say something!"

"Hi, yes, it's me, Samantha Mackenzie. Yep, in the flesh. Okay. Bye," she said, then handed the phone back to the girl and followed her parents into her new room. She wondered what her new roommate, a Mia Thompson from Arkansas, daughter of Janet and Kyle Thompson, would be like.

Hopefully someone who didn't want her to speak into a cell phone to various family members.

Samantha's shoulders sagged slightly as they walked inside. Except for the regulation twin beds and matching wooden desks and dressers, the room was empty.

"That's odd," her mother said, frowning. "They're supposed to be here by now."

As President and First Lady of the United States, Sam's parents never, ever had to deal with lateness. No one ever kept them waiting for anything—a table at a restaurant, a meeting with their staffs, even a doctor's appointment.

"I once heard this rumor, Mom, that there are people who don't keep a minute-by-minute schedule," Samantha said, widening her eyes for effect.

Her mother played along. "How do they live?"

Liz was in the hall, talking into her cell phone. She pulled it away from her ear. "Roommate's caught in traffic. Estimated time of arrival, ten minutes."

Sam nodded, then watched as her father placed her things on the bed by the window. She shook her head and picked them up again and moved them to the other bed. "She should at least get the good bed if she has to live with me," she explained, smiling ruefully.

"Has Liz gone over the itinerary?" her father asked her in the same tone he used when dealing with his chiefs of staff.

"For?" Sam said, playing dumb. Really, though, she felt hurt. Did he have to use the word "itinerary" here? Today?

Her mother cleared her throat. "There are just a few small functions your father and I were hoping you'd . . . enjoy attending?"

"You're so cute when you act like I have a choice," Samantha said quietly, crossing her arms. "After this, one event per week, nothing requiring heels or a skirt suit."

Her mother kissed her on the cheek as Liz poked her head in again, nodding to the President and pointing to her watch.

"Honey—" her father began, his it's-time-to-leave look on his face—and on Liz's.

Suddenly being on her own seemed kind of frightening. "Already?" Sam said, trying to hide her disappointment. "You wore jeans," she said, trying to think of something to prolong their stay. "You, uh, you should at least assemble a bookcase."

"As if you're not chomping at the bit to get rid of us," her father said with a knowing smile.

Samantha blinked, trying to hold in the tears. "The President and the First Lady, yes. My mom and dad—not as much."

Then she pretended to shoo them away. "Go, get out of here. You've got a campaign to run."

As they walked outside to say goodbye, surrounded by Secret Service agents, a crowd encircled the waiting motorcade.

"And on three, two, one," Sam muttered to herself. Right on cue, the band struck up "Hail to the Chief."

"Remember," her mother whispered into her ear as they hugged goodbye, "a full load of laundry dries faster than a nearly empty one, always take the stairs, don't sweat the petty things—"

"And don't pet the sweaty things," her father added with a wink.

Her mother held Sam at arm's length and looked into her eyes. "Your father will be back next week, campaigning."

"So if you need anything . . . just call Liz," he told her.

Sam managed a smile. "I'll be fine, Mom. But thanks." Her mom kissed her cheek. Then her father came over.

"Well, how about that . . ." The President

broke off and scratched his clean-shaven chin. "I'm at a loss for words."

"Just tell me you'll miss me," Sam whispered as her father hugged her close.

"When the election's over, we're gonna spend time together," he promised. "A whole day—twenty-four hours."

"In a row?" Sam mumbled, only half-joking.

"I promise," her father said. Then he let go and his security detail formed a protective barrier around him. Her mother wiped away a few tears and hugged her once more.

"Without you in Washington, it's just a job," Liz told Sam, giving her a heartfelt hug. "Goodbye, Sam."

Sam's heart squeezed. This was much harder than she'd ever expected. "Bye, Liz."

And within moments, everything was back to normal—at least as normal as it ever was for Sam. Her father's special security detail retreated and the snipers withdrew from the rooftops. Policemen got back into their patrol cars and drove off while National Guardsmen folded up their barricades, loading them onto trucks. Even the marching band marched off, still playing "Hail to the Chief."

"Well, I guess I'm alone at last," Samantha said under her breath. She heard someone cough behind her. "Well, as alone as I ever am," she said, turning to see the two Secret Service agents in charge of her detail, Agents Bock and Dylan, directing some other agents to their posts.

"Please be mellow," Samantha pleaded with Bock and Dylan as they took their positions on either side of her dorm room door.

Agent Bock studied her. He was an ace agent—and a pain in the butt. "On one condition," he said. "Could we major in something fun? I'm really hoping we're not premed . . . and light on the math."

"Zip it, Bock," Sam said. She turned to the permanently poker-faced Dylan. "But especially you, Dylan. Not another word, okay?" Then she closed the door in their faces. *I wonder what Bock would do if I registered for advanced biophysics?*

Okay. Now she really was alone. Taking a deep breath, she walked over to the window, reaching up to unfasten the sturdy metal lock. She pushed lightly on the bulletproof glass, then opened the window and leaned out, breathing in the late-afternoon air.

"Oh!" she said, startled to see Secret Service agents Colvin and Mercer staring right back at her from the dorm window next door. She ducked back inside and the agents did too. And then, like that old *I Love Lucy* episode where Lucy imitates a mime, she leaned out once more—and so did they.

Frustrated, Sam walked away from the window and began to unpack. She'd gone on a major shopping spree with Liz a few weeks ago, and seeing all the neatly folded T-shirts, shorts, and jeans that they'd selected together made her feel slightly homesick.

A sarcastic voice coming from outside interrupted her.

"Hey, if you're gonna look through my stuff, at least help me carry it."

The door flew open and there stood a pretty girl with long black hair that framed her face, her slender arms loaded down with stuffed-to-the-max duffel bags. She wore tight jeans and an itsy-bitsy halter top that would have fit Samantha in first grade. The girl looked over at the agents and rolled her brown eyes.

Sam hurried over. "Let me help you. Men, right?"

The girl studied her. "So you *are* aware of the two large individuals with stun guns, sticky hands"—she broke off to call out the door, "and no manners," then turned back to Sam— "flanking our door?"

Samantha smiled. "You must be Mia."

Mia looked closer at her, and a look of realization passed over her face. She fumbled in one of her bags and pulled out a crumpled computer printout. "But I'm guessing you aren't Linda, redhead, Paterson, New Jersey. Plays trombone?"

Samantha shook her head and stuck her hands in her back pockets. "They made a last-minute roommate switch," she said apologetically. "Security reasons. They were supposed to contact you . . ." From the look on Mia's face, Sam realized that hadn't happened. "They didn't contact you."

"That wasn't a joke?" Mia asked, dazed. "I thought it was one of my stupid friends playing around."

Sam threw her hands into the air. "Surprise!" She held out her hand, unable to shake the years of formal introductions ingrained in her behavior. "My name's Samantha Mack—"

"You're not quite as tall in person," Mia interrupted.

Sam took a deep breath. This wasn't going quite the way she had hoped. "So, I'm really excited about this year. There are so many things I want to do."

"No offense, Miss Mackenzie," Mia started.

"Samantha," Sam corrected with a friendly smile.

Mia tried again. "I have a plan, Saman-tha. For college."

"That's great!" Samantha said excitedly, glad to know that she had a roommate who was on the same page as she was. "I'll prob-ably major in economics with a focus on industrial organization, definitely study abroad, not Oxford. I'll save that for post-grad work."

Suddenly Sam realized that she was do-ing all the talking while Mia was doing all the listening—with an expression of bewil-dered horror on her face.

"My plan was to have fun," Mia said slowly.

Sam felt her cheeks redden. "Oh, that's in my plan too."

Mia bent to pick up her things. "I'm sorry, I just want to have a normal college experience."

Sam stopped her. "All I want is normal, Mia," she implored. Sam had a good feeling about this girl. She seemed bright and con-fident—just the type of person Sam had hoped to be paired up with. She couldn't let her just walk out and risk getting paired up with Linda the redheaded trombone player.

"I should go to the housing office," Sam said, not moving.

Mia stood there, wavering.

"They said you're the kind of girl who's up for anything."

"What's that?"

"The housing office," Sam bluffed. "After they finally found a roommate who checked out . . ."

"I guess that means the shoplifting thing got cleared up," Mia mumbled.

"'Mia's your woman,' they said. 'An adventurer,' they called you," Sam said, laying it on thick. "I'm disappointed."

"You're manipulating me," Mia accused.

Sam hung her head. "Yes."

"It's kind of working," Mia admitted, a hint of a smile playing on her lips.

"Please, Mia, just give it a chance. That's all I'm asking."

Mia was softening. "I guess this situation could have its advantages."

"Absolutely," Samantha blurted out. "Like, in case of a national emergency, guess who gets the free seat on the chopper?"

Mia smirked. "I was thinking your Secret Service agents could get us beer."

"Forget it," came Bock's deep voice from out in the hallway.

"We'll work on it," Sam whispered conspiratorially.

To Sam's relief, Mia dumped her bags back on the floor and extended her hand. "Mia Thompson. Arkansas royalty."

"I didn't know they had royalty in . . . Arkansas," Sam said uncertainly.

"Of course they do," Mia said. "My dad's a king—the Tire King, best seller in the South. Sadly, there have been several queens since my mom." She straightened her shoulders, moving on. "If we're gonna cohabitate, you really must let me do your brows."

"Uh, sure." Sam's hand flew to her forehead. "Just don't let my agents see you pointing anything sharp at me. They may overreact."

"Would that involve tackling me?" Mia's face lit up. "The bald one's sexy."

"You can forget that, too," Bock called out.

Mia surveyed the room. "Bonus points for giving me the good bed—I like you already."

Sam smiled. Score one for her, minus one for Dad.

"But a few ground rules," Mia continued. "Starting with—don't kiss my ass, because I certainly won't be kissing yours."

This was music to Sam's ears. "Mia, I like you already."

Mia plopped down on a mattress. "I can't wait to inspect all the fishies in our new sea. But for you, it's probably more like an aquarium, huh?"

Sam gave her a confused look.

"Fishbowl?" Mia prompted. "People staring at you?"

"Once people get to know me, they're pretty normal around me," Sam allowed, sitting down beside her. Now Mia was the one giving her a look. "What?"

"People who are normal don't have to

say 'people are normal around me.'" She pushed herself up. "Now let's get you changed so we can hit some parties."

"Actually, my night's kind of scheduled," Sam explained, wondering what was wrong with her black pants and crisp white shirt. "But I thought I looked okay. No?"

Mia shrugged. "Sure . . . if you're hanging out with the dean."

Sam tried not to laugh.

Because that was exactly what was on her schedule.

The dean's house was elegantly furnished. The lavish buffet was filled with fancy hors d'oeuvres, and white-shirted waiters manned large chafing dishes of roast beef and ham. The crowd was well dressed, well educated, and well connected.

And Samantha found herself wishing she were anywhere but here—like at the keg party she had passed along the way.

"Miss Mackenzie, I speak for the entire faculty when I welcome you to Redmond, and assure you that you'll be treated just like any student," the dean said as the crowd hushed to listen, "just the minute we conclude this elaborate party in your honor."

She did her best to circulate among the faculty members, smiling politely and engaging in a few halfhearted conversations. A particularly boring professor cornered her by the punch bowl. As he began to discuss the United States' economic policies, Sam stared out the window.

"Of course, the fundamental importance of agenda control was established . . . ," he droned.

Suddenly, Sam snapped to attention. Outside the window was a huge banner that read FUN . . . THIS WAY, complete with an arrow. And there stood Mia, waving to her with a group of other students.

Samantha grinned. Now, this was what college was all about.

"In the sense that they would support

their preferred policy," the professor rambled on.

Sam glanced over at Agents Bock and Dylan. How would they react to FUN . . . THIS WAY? *Probably not very well*, she thought, downcast. She looked back at Mia and gave her a slight shake of her head. "Sorry," she mouthed.

Mia shook her head too and motioned once more for Sam to come. Sam shrugged, tilting her head toward the Secret Service. Finally, Mia and the other kids disappeared into the California night.

Exactly where I want to be.

chapter**four**

Later that night, after the party at the dean's house, Samantha sat for a while next to a pond near her dorm. It would have been very peaceful . . . if she hadn't had four Secret Service agents looming over her.

Samantha had always been the ideal First Daughter. Whether she was living in the Governor's Mansion or the White House, she knew she had always made her parents proud. And it wasn't that she didn't want to keep on doing that. It was just that, well, she needed a little room to grow up. To live. Experience what college was all about.

And that's not going to happen with you guys around me, she thought wearily as she pushed herself off the cold stone bench and trudged back to her dorm room.

She tried her key in the door, but it wouldn't open. It was locked from the inside. Which meant—

"You missed a great party," Mia whispered, pulling the door open a crack. Her hair was rumpled, and her rose-colored lipstick was smudged.

"Sorry about that," Sam said, wondering who else was inside.

"Fortunately I can provide another normal college experience—in which the roommate kicks you out in the name of truly higher education." Mia pulled the door open wider to reveal a cute college guy wearing a Redmond T-shirt sprawled out on her bed. He gave Sam a wave.

Samantha swallowed. She wasn't expecting this to happen so fast. "Can I just get my—"

Mia held up her fingers. "Come back in a few."

"Minutes?" Sam said in dismay.

Mia looked back at the guy. "Hours."

Sam blinked, surprised, as Mia shut the door in her face. Bock and Dylan raised their eyebrows as Sam shrugged it off and headed down to the TV room. No way was she going to let on to her security detail that this bothered her.

No way was she going to give them an excuse to send her home.

The TV room was deserted. Sam plopped down on a ratty old couch, picked up the remote, and began flipping aimlessly through the channels. She pretended not to notice as Bock and Dylan sat down in the chairs beside her. CNN, MSNBC, *The Tonight Show with Jay Leno*, *Late Show with David Letterman* . . . all of them were talking about the same thing: Samantha Mackenzie's first day of college.

Ugh. It was too depressing. She flipped some more and decided to watch the Home Shopping Network. They were discussing a particularly interesting form of hair removal that Sam might need one day. *After all, my brows obviously need serious tending to,* she thought, frowning.

A few seconds later, Dylan cleared his throat. With a sigh, Sam picked up the remote again and changed the channel to ESPN. She looked over to them and they gave her a smile and a thumbs-up. Rummaging in her purse, she pulled out a paperback and began to read.

"Samantha Mackenzie?"

Sam looked up to see two cute guys standing in front of her. She put down her book.

"Greetings, Ms. Mackenzie," said Cutie #1. "The Redmond chapter of Sigma Chi is pleased to invite you to our Annual Plunge."

"An invitation-only event," Cutie #2 added.

Samantha cocked an eyebrow.

"Bathing suits are mandatory," Cutie #1 said. "Bikinis are preferred." He smiled salaciously.

"Oh, thanks a lot, guys," Samantha said drolly. But secretly she was excited at the thought. Her very first frat party!

Cutie #2 gave a low bow. "We hope to see you there, Ms. Mackenzie."

"How do you look in a bikini, Bock?" Samantha said as the Secret Service agent pretended to be very engrossed in some football stats. He considered her question, then gave her a "so-so" motion with his hands.

Seeing her starched-shirt security detail in a pair of swim trunks would almost be worth the price of tuition.

Classes at Redmond were thrilling. It felt so great to be in a real college classroom, listening to a real college professor lecture.

"'They had already poured the sum total of their knowledge into his waiting vessel; and the vessel was not full, his intellect was not satisfied, his soul was not at peace, his heart was not still.'"

Sam scribbled away in her notebook, determined not to miss a single word.

"Ladies and gentlemen, I shall do my best to see to it that your intellect is satisfied, your soul is at peace, and your vessel is filled this semester," the professor said, his voice gravelly. "For starters, would it be possible to shift your attention to me? I know I'm not as pretty, but come on."

Slowly, Sam looked up. The entire class was whispering and staring at her as if she were a specimen in the biology lab. The seats around her were empty. The closest people to her were her Secret Service agents.

Can I crawl into a hole and die? she thought, beyond embarrassed as she feigned fascination with something in her book.

"Excuse me, Professor, I didn't see anything on the syllabus about a vessel."

The professor looked to see who was speaking. The speaker was tall, dark blond, and very, very gorgeous. Sam sat up straighter.

Gorgeous consulted a copy of his class syllabus, apparently perplexed. "I see the books I need to buy, but there's no mention of a vessel of any kind, and you said you were gonna fill one, right?"

Now people were beginning to snicker, rolling their eyes in Gorgeous's direction. He was oblivious.

The professor gave him a bewildered stare.

No one was looking at Sam any longer.

He said that on purpose, she realized, turning to look at him. *He saved me!* A fact that was confirmed when Gorgeous gave her a subtle wink with one of his beautiful green eyes.

When class let out, there was no way she could just let him walk away. "Excuse me!" she called out, jogging after him.

When he turned around, she gulped. He was even more gorgeous up close, with his tousled hair and gold-flecked green eyes.

"I just wanted to thank you for rescuing me back there," Sam said sheepishly, scuffing her shoe along the ground.

"It was nothing," Gorgeous said, offering her a lopsided grin. The sleeves on his red shirt were rolled up to reveal muscular, lightly tanned arms. "Anyway, you don't strike me as a person who needs rescuing."

The idea that he thought she was capable of taking care of herself made her stand up straighter. "I'm Samantha," she said, smiling. Before he could respond, she rushed on. "I know—I'm taller in person, fatter, thinner, fill in the blank." She let out her breath. "I get that."

Gorgeous hefted his book bag over his shoulder. "Actually, I was gonna say you look exactly like I thought you would." His lips formed a slow smile. "Bye, Samantha." And then he turned and headed out across the grassy quad.

Samantha was still standing there, trying to come up with something semi-intelligent to say—*See you later! My hero! Thanks again!*—when Mia jogged up beside her.

She settled for a small wave goodbye.

"Not bad, Ms. Mackenzie," Mia said approvingly.

"You really shouldn't objectify men like that, Mia," Samantha scolded. Her face lit up. "Besides, he's mine. I saw him first."

"Fair enough."

A passing student waved excitedly at Sam. "Hi, Samantha!"

"Nice to meet you too!" Mia called out, rolling her eyes.

chapter**five**

Convertibles, SUVs, and snazzy sports cars were parked haphazardly over the lawn of Sigma Chi House. Music blasted from speakers the size of refrigerators. Guys in swim trunks loped by, carrying six-packs and liquor bottles, sunlight dancing on well-toned abs. Suntanned sorority girls who looked like they had stepped out of a PacSun ad languished on chaise lounges.

I can't believe I'm at a fraternity party! Samantha thought as she and Mia crossed the lush green lawn toward the large land-scaped pool, beach totes slung across their shoulders. *So this is why parents spend their life savings to send their children to college.* She checked the string on her bright blue bikini for the fifteenth time. Being grilled by seasoned reporters under 100-kilowatt lightbulbs was nothing compared to how exposed she felt now. *My father would kill me if he saw me walking around like this!* she thought, a mixture of fear and glee blending in her blood.

"Just so we're clear, I've never been a 'plus one' before," Mia said with a sniff, referring to her tagalong status. "And it doesn't agree with me." Not only was she curvier than Sam, her bikini was tinier. Heads swiveled as they paused next to the pool, and for once, Sam had a pretty good hunch that it wasn't because her father was the President.

Sam shot her friend an appreciative look. "Thanks for coming, Mia." She never could have come here by herself. She almost couldn't believe she'd come even with reinforcement.

Mia smacked her gloss-slicked lips. "I can't believe how cute these guys are."

"I can't believe I'm not wearing a robe," Sam whispered, looking down at her cleavage. "The last time I got to go to a party like this, I could only fill out a ruffled bikini."

"Focus, Sam," Mia instructed, her eyes flitting from guy to guy. "We're at a frat party."

Sam squared her bare shoulders. "You're right. This is fantastic. I think I'm really blending in, too."

Mia nodded. "Absolutely."

Then they both glanced back at the swim-trunk-clad Secret Service agents standing behind them. The men did not look at all pleased.

"I don't suppose there's any chance the hairy Olsen twins could back off?" Mia whispered.

Samantha frowned and gave a small shake of her head.

Mia rubbed her hands together. "In that case, let me show you how to make a real entrance."

Samantha watched in shocked admiration as her friend made a beeline for the diving board. Mia walked purposefully to the end. She stood up straight, stretched her arms overhead, rose up on her tiptoes, and—

Splash! Executed a perfect cannonball into the water.

Sam had a feeling that Mia thought this was going to get her big results. There were a few hoots and hollers, but most of the guys—all the hot ones included—had swarmed around Samantha the instant she'd taken a seat on a vacant poolside chair.

I'm used to connecting with people like press secretaries and diplomats, Sam thought anxiously, looking at the smiling faces around her. Connecting with regular college students? That was much, much harder.

She politely declined a cup of beer and shot an apologetic look at Mia.

"Don't worry about me," Mia said to the guys, who remained oblivious to her charms. "I don't even have a name. Just call me 'Sam's friend.'"

Sam spotted the frat guys who had in-

Midnight snack, White House style.

The First Family.

A proud papa.

Saying goodbye to the Washington press corps.

As if being a freshman weren't scary enough . . .

Sam's first frat party.

News
travels fast
when
you're the
President's
daughter.

James.

A day of freedom with James.

Will the paparazzi ever let Sam live a normal life?

The belle of the ball and her prince.

Making a grand entrance.

On the campaign trail.

Sam takes a moment for herself.

vited her coming toward her in flag-themed boxer shorts. She put her hand to her mouth, trying not to laugh as they performed a raunchy dance to "Hail to the Chief." *This sure gives new meaning to the song*, Sam thought as the guys gyrated around her. Suddenly she was lifted high into the air, chair and all. Four very strong and very cute frat guys were hoisting her up as if she were the bride in a Jewish wedding.

"That's enough!" she cried, giggling. "Put me down! I mean it!" But of course she didn't.

The guys carried her around the party and Sam held on tight to the armrests, excitement and anxiety zooming through her. Not only would falling off the chair majorly hurt, it would be disastrous for her reputation on campus. *Did you see the President's daughter fall on her butt at Sigma Chi?*

"No way she actually gets thrown in," a snotty-looking girl muttered as Sam and the guys passed by.

Why were people so mean? Didn't they

get that for the first time in her life, she was actually having a normal teenage experience?

Forget them, she decided, laughing as the guys trotted her toward the deep end. No one was going to take this feeling away from her.

"Enough. Put me down!" she ordered, laughing.

"One, two—" the guys began to chant. One of them reached into his pocket and pulled something out.

What is that? she thought, squinting in the sunlight as he pointed it toward her. *It can't be a—*

"Gun!" shouted Bock and Dylan.

Before Samantha could blink, the Secret Service agents had tackled the unsuspecting frat guy to the ground. More agents— ones wearing suits and ties—stormed in, grabbing Sam off the chair.

"But—" she protested as they put her on the ground and shielded her with their bodies. From her place on the bottom of the pile, she watched with horror as even more agents swooped in, guns drawn. Fraternity boys and sorority girls were screaming, scattering over hedges and running into the frat house.

A fleet of black SUVs jounced to a halt around the perimeter of the pool. Sam felt herself being pulled up, and a few seconds later she was tossed in the backseat of one of the cars. She frantically searched through the window for Mia, locating her lying spread-eagled on the empty, trashed lawn. The driver peeled off, the force throwing her back against the cool black leather seat.

"It was a water gun," she whispered, barely able to believe what had just happened. "A water gun."

An hour later, Samantha's mortification had had time to simmer into downright anger. Still clad in only her bikini and white sandals, she marched down the hall of the California campaign headquarters, turning down an offer of a towel and refusing to let anyone get in her way.

"I'm sorry, I'd have more on, but I

wasn't exactly given time to get my stuff!" she said with a huff.

Inside the presidential suite, she was momentarily happy to see Liz Pappas. But then her blood picked up boiling where it had left off. Her father—the man responsible for ruining her very first college party, and most likely her entire college experience—was behind the heavy mahogany doors that Liz was so zealously guarding.

And he had some serious explaining to do.

"Don't tell me he's too busy," Sam told Liz, stomping her foot. "I need to talk to him. Where is he?"

Liz looked pale. "Wow, you look great in that. What's going on?"

"He's got too many Secret Service agents following me around. I can't take it!"

As usual, Liz tried to smooth things over. "Election year, Sam. Tension is high. Just take a breath and let me handle it." She quietly opened the inner chamber door and tiptoed in. "Mr. President?" Then she disappeared inside.

Sam waited impatiently, too mad to think straight—and too mad to react to the raised eyebrows of the people who could see her from inside the suite. A water gun? The Secret Service tackled a frat boy for a water gun? This was going way too far.

Liz reappeared. "It's not a good time."

Sam could feel her blood pressure rise. "Fine, just tell him I'll ditch the whole college thing and become a Hooters girl. Good benefits, I hear."

Liz held her breath and went back inside the chamber. A minute later, Sam's father appeared in the doorway. "Man, I came close to wearing the same bikini today," he quipped, making the onlookers laugh.

Sam crossed her arms in front of her as her father took her to the side for a private conversation.

"If you want your daughter to have friends, we need to make some changes," Samantha whispered hotly.

Her father shook his head. "Sorry, I don't negotiate with people in swimwear."

Didn't he see that this was so not a time for jokes? "When Chelsea was at Stanford, her Secret Service backed off," Samantha reminded him. "They blended in. They wore Birkenstocks."

"I don't know, Sam—navy blue suits with Birkenstocks? You sure you want that?" Then he grew serious. "It was a whole different time, Sam," her father said, as he had so many times before. "It's a whole different world now."

Samantha could feel a lump forming in her throat. "Look, Dad, it's not like I'm drunk and sleeping around," she said, her voice cracking. "Come on, Dad. I know you were my age once. All I'm asking for is a shred of normalcy. I can't even go to a party with my friends."

"You're right. You can't."

She looked at him, dressed to perfection in his tailored suit, his slightly graying hair combed just so, a resigned expression on his face.

Who was she kidding? Things were never going to change for her. "Forget it," she said, pulling away from his hold and walking out of the suite.

Why couldn't my father be an accountant? she thought as she strode down the hallway. *Or a teacher? Or an engineer? Something completely regular. Something—*

"Go back to school." Liz had caught up to her. For some reason, her brown eyes were sparkling.

"What?"

"I just spoke with your father and you're on a new diet—social security lite. Have fun—just not too much."

Sam squealed. "Thank you!" she said, throwing her arms around Liz. "Thank you so much!" Somehow Liz had managed to get through to her father.

And that meant . . . she was practically free!

chapter**six**

When the SUV dropped her back at Woody House, Bock and Dylan were still there. But just Bock and Dylan. No more suits positioned behind trees, no more agents camped out in the bushes.

Just two guys in casual clothes that she could tolerate.

"And then there were two!" Sam said, gratefully accepting the blazer Bock offered her. She had had enough humiliation for one day. To her utter joy, the agents accompanied her to her floor—but took seats in the lobby and waved her off, letting her go to her room by herself.

She unlocked the door and stepped inside. Then she hurried over to the window, unlocked it, and stuck her head outside. No one! She was 100 percent alone.

"Finally," she breathed, collapsing on the bed.

A little while later, after she had showered and dressed, Mia returned, and after Sam told her the sordid details—and joyous outcome—of her visit to her father, they headed out to have some fun.

"Lunge at me," Samantha said to her roommate, pretending to dodge imaginary punches. Mia had been in serious pout mode over the ruined frat party, but her anger hadn't lasted long. "Hit me. Tackle me. Come on, you know you want to."

She blinked with surprise as Mia pushed up her sleeves, backed up, and prepared to take a running start.

"Or we could just celebrate," Sam said quickly. The freedom of her downsized security detail was irresistible. "I've narrowed it down to three target areas, which if hit quickly—"

Right then a burst of cheering shattered the calm night air.

"Or maybe it's right under our noses," Sam said excitedly. "What's going on there?" She jogged toward the commotion.

"Sam, I don't think that's a party," Mia called after her.

Sam slowed to a stop as she reached the crowd that had gathered on campus. People held handmade signs in the air. SAMUELS FOR PRESIDENT. CHANGE OUR LEADERSHIP NOW! It was a political rally for her father's opponent.

And she was right in the middle of it.

Students around her began to whisper and point in her direction. She tried not to pay them any attention, curious to hear what the rally leader was saying into his bullhorn.

"While Mackenzie racks up his frequent-flier miles, Samuels is right here, right now," the excited young man told the crowd. "At home." The crowd stirred, nodding.

"Health care, education, new jobs—just

a few of the things Samuels has been working on, while Mackenzie's been out of the office, out of the country, taking money out of our pockets," he went on. "Next step, out of office!"

Sam's blood boiled. She was used to people talking trash about her father—it came with the job—but she wasn't used to hearing it in person. Her cheeks flamed. From behind her she heard Mia start to heckle the rally leader. She appreciated her friend's efforts, but—

"Samantha Mackenzie," the young man said, spotting her in the crowd. "How good of you to join us. Ladies and gentlemen, how about some good ol' bipartisan debate. Ms. Mackenzie?"

Sam felt like a deer in the headlights as she glanced uncertainly at the faces around her. She wanted to defend her father, but getting up in front of a crowd of her classmates to deliver an unplanned retort wasn't exactly high on her list. She looked helplessly over at Mia, hoping her friend would help her slink away.

But Mia would have none of that. "Get on up there," she whispered, motioning her forward.

"What do you say, Samantha?" the rally leader needled her. "Daddy's not here—can we hear what you have to say or do you only do what Daddy tells you?"

Sam froze. She couldn't do it. She turned on her heel and fled.

"Another Mackenzie running from the real issues," the rally leader called after her. "Like father, like daughter."

The sounds of their sandals made soft squishing noises against the grass as they walked up Rose Hill, two Secret Service agents several yards behind them. "What was that about?" Mia asked, crossing her arms.

"Freedom of speech," Sam said briskly, her eyes glued forward. She avoided Mia's pointed stare. "They have the right to express their beliefs."

"The freedom goes both ways," Mia

said, exasperated. "Why don't you get to speak your mind?"

"Sometimes you just have to stop and count to ten," Sam said, taking small gulps of the cool night air. How could she explain to Mia how it felt to have to squash her opinions . . . that sometimes being the daughter of the President was harder than *being* the President?

"Sure," Mia cracked. "Next time I steal your pretzel sticks at snack time, I'll do that."

Samantha stopped. "Fine, wanna know what I think? I think my father's administration gives a great deal of attention to its domestic agenda," she declared. "Take his college-tuition tax exemption proposal—"

"Blah, blah, blah." Mia rolled her eyes. "Hard to get that stuff out of your head, huh?"

Sam shrugged. When you lived and breathed the real-life *West Wing* for as long as she had, it kind of was.

"Only one thing I can think of to help," Mia said.

"What's that?"

Mia pointed to a steep hill that lay in front of them. "Something like that."

The hill was soaking wet, and a lit sign above it read FRESHMEN TAKE A DIVE. Tents with food and stalls set up by various student organizations on campus were along the side. People were sliding down the hill with plastic bags, rubber garbage-can lids— anything that moved. Everyone was covered in mud, lots of them appeared to be drunk, and most of them were screaming like crazy.

It looked like the dirtiest, funnest thing ever.

The girls walked over to the departure point. A few people glanced curiously at them—and at the security detail.

Sam hesitated, glancing down at her shorts and top. "I should change," she said, trying to come up with an excuse for why she shouldn't participate. "I don't want to ruin my outfit."

Mia stepped behind her, putting her hands on her shoulders. "Mud can only improve it, lady." She picked up two garbage can lids, handed one to Sam, and launched herself down the hill on her own, shrieking with delight.

Sam hung back. She turned to look for her security detail, which stood far behind her. The agents gave her a small encouraging wave.

You wanted your freedom and now you have it, Sam thought, closing her eyes. *So don't be afraid to take it.*

She clutched the garbage can lid to her chest and ran forward, leaped into the air, and landed.

Except she didn't move. *Leave it to me to be the one person who gets stuck in the mud,* she thought, standing back up. This time, she was determined. Focusing, she ran forward and tried it again. This time she flew down the hill the way Mia had.

It was terrifying.

Her lid bucked this way and that, whizzing her past her fellow students, spattering mud on her legs and arms. Suddenly she hit a bump and her arms flew up and off the lid. And then she was flying through the air into a tsunami of mud.

She landed hard, slamming directly into a fellow slider.

Sam gaped. It was none other than Gorgeous himself.

Somehow Gorgeous recognized her under her crusting mask of mud. "Are you okay?" he asked worriedly. "Did you get the wind knocked out of you?"

She had! And her body seemed to realize this for the first time. She began to snort and howl and wheeze all at once. She gasped as Mia sloshed up beside her, slapping her on the back.

"Do you have a medical condition I should know about, Sam?" she whispered.

"Sam, right, I'm Sam," Samantha choked out, smiling over at Gorgeous. He was even cuter when he was muddy. "I'm so sorry!"

"James," Gorgeous said, "and it was my pleasure." He winced. "But did I hurt you?"

"Yes, a little," Sam confessed, her heart pounding. "You're already muddy—let's go!" She ran up the hill. "You coming or not?"

Mia let out a whoop, James scrambled to his feet, and the three of them took off.

Sam slept like a log that night. In fact, she would have slept until noon if Liz Pappas hadn't phoned at ten a.m. and ordered her to check out the *New York Post* online.

Sam quickly got online and pulled up the site. "No," she gasped, the image waking her up in a hurry. It was a huge photograph of her as she stood, covered in mud, next to Mia—who was clad in nothing but a mud-spattered thong! The caption above it read, "Daddy's Dirty Girl!"

"Oh, man," Sam mumbled. She had seen some people taking pictures last night, but she'd never expected this. It had all been completely innocent—Mia's pants had slid off after a wild slide down the hill—but it sure didn't look innocent.

Mia woke up and padded over in her bare feet. A fur-trimmed sleep mask was pushed on top of her head. "Oh, man," she echoed. Her eyes lit up. "I made the *Post*!"

As Mia did a little celebratory dance, Sam squeezed her eyes shut.

"Suffice it to say," Liz said, "your father feels that he gave you an inch and you took a mile." She paused. "Listen, Sam, you can't pull a stunt like this again. That's me talking."

"I'm so sorry," Sam whispered.

Mia rolled her eyes and motioned for her to hang up. "I don't care who you're groveling to, the great thing about college is that you can hang up."

Sam waved her away. "Put him on," she told Liz boldly.

Mia clapped heartily.

"Are you crazy?" Liz's voice was a squeak. "He's on fire!"

"Look, I'll say, 'Dad, I love you. This is unfortunate. But I'm not going to apologize for a bunch of college kids being college kids.'" She swallowed. She liked the way that sounded. But Liz was silent. "Hello?"

The voice that replied wasn't Liz's. "I'm listening."

"Oh, hi, Dad," Sam said, startled. "Listen, I'm really sorry," she backpedaled, her pulse speeding up.

"What are you thinking, Sam?" he asked in a way that made Sam's heart sink.

"I know."

"Your partner in crime—I take it she's a new friend?"

"Yes," Sam said quickly. "That's my roommate, Mia."

"Just to be clear—she's the one in the thong?"

Sam swallowed. "Correct, the one in the thong."

"Put her on, Sam."

Sam offered the phone to Mia. "He wants to talk to you."

Mia backed up, shaking her head.

"Now," Sam said.

Reluctantly, Mia took a deep breath and put the phone to her ear. "Mr. President, this is Mia Thompson, and with all due respect, while your diplomatic skills are top-notch, I think you need some parenting advice."

Sam cringed as Mia listened to her father. This was not going to go well. But to her surprise, Mia soon had a contrite expression on her face. "Yes, sir. Of course," Mia said. "I see your point."

Whatever the President was telling her, it was working. Mia seemed to be completely won over.

"Yeah, you too, sir," Mia said a minute later. "Thank you. Oh, and good job on that China thing, by the way."

She gave Sam a small, sheepish smile as she hung up the phone. "Wow. He's good."

Sam was dumbstruck. "Yes, he is."

"The difference is, he's my president, Sam. But he's your father."

"Not when he's calling from the Oval Office, he's not," Sam said, throwing herself down on her bed.

"Oval Office, Shmoval Office—every father's gotta learn to let their little girl go at some point." Mia sat down beside her. "And every little girl's gotta let go of her father."

Sam looked at her, shaking off a yawn. "And how do you do that when you never really had him to begin with?"

chapter**seven**

Sam spent the next day holed up in the dorm's study room, surrounded by notebooks and highlighters and thick textbooks. Finally, though, she couldn't stand reading about the Renaissance any longer—she needed a cold beverage and she needed it now.

As she grabbed a soda from the machine on her floor, she paused to look out the hallway's large glass windows. What she saw made her stop in her tracks.

Legions of press were camped outside the building. Reporters milled about, photographers were setting up their cameras, and curious students were gathering to watch.

"Shoot," Sam muttered, moving away from the window before anyone spotted her. Why did the press want to hound her like this? It made no sense. She ran back down the hall to her room and jiggled the doorknob. One of Mia's socks was wrapped around it.

"You've gotta be kidding me," Sam muttered, trying the knob again. "Mia!" she yelled. "I'm locked out. Mia? You getting a Ph.D. in there? I need your help."

After several seconds of frantic pounding and zero response, Sam took off down the hall. She knocked on every door she passed, trying without success to find someone home—or at least someone who had left their door unlocked.

From the nearby stairwell she heard voices and footsteps coming up.

In a last-ditch effort, she ran to the door at the end of the hallway marked RA. To her relief, it was open.

"Phew," Sam said, leaning against the

doorway. And then she looked up. None other than Gorgeous himself was sitting at a desk.

"You?" Sam managed to say, flustered. "This—this is the RA's room."

"Yes," James said. "Good thing I'm the RA, then."

"What happened to Stuart?" Sam asked, hardly believing her luck.

"Stuart preferred something a bit lower-key," James said, revealing a flash of dimple. "He'll be over in the C Wing."

"Oh," Sam said, trying not to look nonplussed. "Sorry to hear that." She heard the voice of what could only be a reporter trying to scout her out coming down the hallway—and the angry voices of Bock and Dylan on his tail.

"So . . . seems you need a place to hide out for a bit," James said, cocking an eyebrow.

Sam's face relaxed into a smile. "Seems I do."

"They have to leave sooner or later, right?" Sam asked, popping another grape in her mouth and looking out the window. She and James had been holed up in his room for some time now—long enough for the press corps to get stools and chairs and make themselves fairly comfortable.

James looked torn. Then his face lit up. "I have a better idea." He pulled off his hooded purple sweatshirt with the blue Redmond logo—and his T-shirt came off as well. Sam could feel her face flushing as he put his T-shirt back on, then handed her his sweatshirt.

"Put this on. Wait right here."

As he went out into the hallway, Sam did as she was told, snuggling into the warm fleece. It smelled of pine and soap, the scent making her toes tingle as she breathed it in.

"Need a tissue?" James asked, popping back inside. An official-looking ring of keys dangled from his fingers.

"No," Sam said, trying to cover up her sweatshirt sniffing. "I'm good."

He grabbed a baseball cap from a hook and tossed it to Sam. She put it on, and he pulled the hood of her sweatshirt up over it.

"Follow me," he said, heading out into the hall. "Ready, Mike?" he called loudly.

Sam walked out, keeping her head down.

"Stay as long as you need to, Sam," James said toward the doorway.

Out of the corner of her eye, Sam spotted Bock down the hall. To her relief, he appeared to be fooled.

They walked down the fire stairs. At the bottom, James used a key to turn off the alarm, then led her out a back door.

She fought off a giggle as they walked right past the clueless press line. As they passed the very last camera, their eyes met—and in unspoken agreement, they began running as fast as they could.

Sam's baseball cap flew off and her long hair fell across her shoulders.

But it didn't matter. They were too far away to be caught now.

They were free.

"You hate it, huh?" James said, eyeing Sam's second slice of pizza.

"It tastes like freedom," Sam said, licking a bit of sauce from her lip. They'd taken refuge in a nearby pizzeria. There were a few other patrons, but no one had paid them any attention.

Sam took another bite, savoring the taste. "I should warn you, I'm a very slow eater. Terrible on the system to rush."

"I can see that," James said with a laugh.

"So there will be plenty of time for discussion," Sam said matter-of-factly. "Starting with the topic of . . . you. Tell me something I don't know."

"Something you don't know . . . okay." He put his slice down. "Brazil is the only country named after a tree. Bagged lettuce that you buy in the store is washed in chlorine."

Sam was impressed. "You didn't answer my question, but still . . . not bad, James." She leaned in conspiratorially. "The little parallelogram above your top lip is called the filtrum. Five years—or half a decade—is a lustrum." She could swap trivia with the best of them. "Beware of a woman who grew up having sleepovers in the Lincoln bedroom," she said by way of explanation. "Chances are her social life was lacking. Lots of time to read."

James looked at her. "Beware of a man whose father was so perfect, his son made it his personal mission to find one thing he didn't know." Then *he* leaned closer. "Every state in the union has a town named Springfield," he rattled off, accepting Sam's challenge. "Male turtles grunt, female turtles hiss."

"Difference between a fruit and a vegetable?" Sam shot back. "Off the vine, fruit ripens, the vegetable just rots."

James extended his arms. "Stretch like so, and middle finger to middle finger, it's equivalent to your height."

Back and forth the facts flew.

"Your ears and nose never—" James began.

"Stop growing," they said in unison. Then they each pushed back in their seats, slightly breathless.

"We are all living Pinocchios," Sam said at last. "But you still haven't told me anything about yourself. Like how you became such a great escape artist."

"Trust me, I'm not that interesting," he said.

Sam begged to differ. "Thanks for doing all this, James," she said quietly.

Something flashed. Sam jerked in her seat. A tiny white-haired old lady stood next to their table. "Excuse me?" she said timidly, holding up a camera. "Otherwise my husband won't believe me."

Sam softened. "Sure."

"And your boyfriend can be in the picture too," the woman offered.

"We're just friends," Sam blurted out quickly. She bit her lip, embarrassed, as James smiled at her.

"You are such a beautiful young lady," the woman told her.

Samantha smiled politely. "Thank you."

"I'm so glad you grew out of that terrible awkward period," the woman confided. She gave Sam's chest a scrutinizing once-over. "And your bosom came in so nicely."

"How about that photo now?" James said impatiently as Sam tried not to look as mortified as she felt.

Maybe James was just a friend for now.

But who knows what he'll be later?

What had started out as awful had turned into a wonderful afternoon. After the pizzeria, Sam and James had walked through the small, lively downtown. No one paid them any attention.

"Really, don't feel obligated to tell me about yourself," Sam kidded as they strolled along the sidewalk. James was such an enigma! He hadn't given her one good tidbit about his life. "Truthfully, one quick call to the FBI or CIA and I can get your blood type, third-grade class picture, and satellite photos of your ex-girlfriends' homes." The scary part was, everything she said was true.

"So I guess that means you didn't find anything when you were looking through my stuff earlier?" James asked, his lips curling into a smile.

Is that just a lucky guess? Sam wondered, cringing at the thought of him catching her sniffing his sweatshirt. "I'll plead the fifth on that," she said. "We'll just start slow. What's your major?"

"That one I can handle. Actuarial science."

Sam blinked. "And what, actually, is actuarial science?" She hoped it didn't have anything to do with funeral homes.

"Statistics, probability," James said. "Assessment of risk. But more importantly, it's what my father did, and what his father did before that, and therefore, what I'm going to do."

He stopped walking, holding up his hand in a silencing motion. "Come on," he said urgently.

"What?" Sam said, confused. Then she

heard the dreaded sound. Running footsteps.

"There she is!" shouted a photographer.
And then there was another. And another.
All running toward them.

She didn't have time to think as James
grabbed her hand.

All she could do was run.

Down side streets, through restaurants,
across the town they ran. One by one, the
photographers dropped off, exhausted. But
one stubborn one hung on.

*Are you that determined to get a picture of
me?* Sam thought, panting, as they ran
down an alley and slid through the back
door of a large brick building.

James led her along a dark, narrow hallway. Sam could hear laughter, then music
swelling. They were in a movie theater.

"Let's do it again," she whispered excitedly.

James shook his head. "Take a breath.
Come here."

They tiptoed into the darkened theater
and slipped into some vacant seats. An old

movie played on the screen. Sam recognized it from the video library at the White House. It was *The Girl Can't Help It,* one of Liz Pappas's favorites.

Sam settled into her chair, a huge smile on her face. The thrill of the chase and the relief at getting away rushed through her. Not to mention that she was in a real movie theater—with no Secret Service! This day totally rocked.

James moved beside her. "Your face," he said softly.

Shoot, did she have pizza sauce on it? She reached up and brushed her skin with her fingers.

James shook his head. "No, the look you get," he said, gazing at her. "It's like when I rode my first bike without training wheels. Like you're experiencing everything for the first time."

"That's because I am," Sam said back. Something was going on between them. Something Sam liked a lot.

The moment was broken when a concession girl walked by and James took a bucket of popcorn from the tray she was holding.

"In that case, you need to try something," he said.

To her surprise, he pulled the popcorn away as she reached for it. "Not so fast," he scolded. He bought a box of Milk Duds, then poured the candy directly on top of the popcorn.

"What are you doing?" Sam asked, semi-repulsed.

"Chocolate snack must be poured directly over popcorn," he said firmly. "That way you get the salty-sweet mixture and some melted chocolate." He smacked his lips. "Sometimes you have to break the rules. You just might get something inspired. Go on, Mackenzie. Break the rules."

Sam hesitated, then slowly helped herself to a tiny handful. She took a tentative bite. She chewed. Not bad. She took another bite. More chewing.

"And?" James prompted.

"And . . . it's disgusting." She grinned, diving in for more. "I love it."

❖❖❖

Back at Woody Hall, Bock stood outside James's room. Inside, Sam sat cross-legged on the floor, asking questions rapid-fire. "Favorite board game?"

"Clue. Favorite season?" James parried.

"Congressional recess. Serena or Venus?"

"Both." James scowled. "Trick question. Favorite dessert?"

"Dinner menu on Thursdays." Sam found herself smiling. "I know I'm not supposed to say this, but back in the White House, my friend Joam makes the most sensational soufflé."

And on and on they went. Sam was dying to know everything she could about James . . . but she was having a harder and harder time keeping her eyes open. The day's events were catching up to her and all she wanted to do was curl up with her soft thermal blanket and sleep.

"Favorite First Daughter joke?" she mumbled sleepily.

"It must be hard," James said.

"It's not so bad." There were so many jokes to choose from—Leno, Letterman, and all the other late-night comedians had at least one a night.

"No, really," James said, and for the first time Sam caught the seriousness in his voice. "It must be hard."

Her eyes snapped open to see James studying her, his features soft.

And for the first time in her life, Sam knew that someone really and truly understood her.

chapter**eight**

Sam bounded down the hallway of Woody House, slowing as she approached James's room. A large white message board was hung on the wall outside his door. Taking a deep breath, she grabbed the marker from its holder and scrawled, "Great night!"

Hmmm, she thought, wondering if that might not be the best thing to write. She wiped the board clean and this time wrote "To My Favorite Escape Artist" instead.

"I could probably leak what you just did

to the press." Sam turned to see a smug-looking guy standing behind her.

"And I could probably have the FBI investigate the amount of porn you download from the Internet."

She smiled as the guy beat a hasty retreat. "Works every time."

As Sam agonized over what to write next, Mia burst into the hall, screeching to a halt beside her. "You're not inviting him to a commitment ceremony," she cracked.

"You're like Secret Service without the secret and without the service. Just annoying." Sam bit her lip. "How do I know that wasn't just a one-time thing? It probably wasn't even a date." After all, James had practically been forced to take such drastic action. Who knew if he even liked her?

"Let's find out." Mia grabbed the pen. "James," she said, reading the words aloud as she wrote them. "Bonfire. Friday night. Be there. Sam."

A huge bonfire illuminated the giant nighttime pep rally as Sam tried to locate James. There were hundreds of people milling about as the football coach pumped up the crowd and the school's mascot—a knight on a horse—put on a show.

"Still no James?" Mia asked, jogging over to her.

Sam shook her head. "Who was I kidding? He's not interested. He was just taking pity on me."

Mia took an optimistic stance. "Give him a little leeway. Between your dad and your portable set of *Men in Black* action figures, the boy's taking on a huge job here."

Sam glanced at Bock and Dylan, standing a few feet behind her. "Oh, please," she said with mock exasperation. "Guys scare so easy. The last guy I liked ran at the first urine request."

"Just like a man," Mia said, playing along. "A little advice, Sam. Always keep your expectations low, and you'll never get burned." She crinkled her forehead. "Anyway, technically, dating your RA is off-limits, isn't it?"

"Sometimes you just have to break the rules, Mia," Sam said with a wink.

Mia smiled, then froze. Her mouth opened, then shut, like a fish gulping for air.

"You all right, Mia?" Sam asked, following her friend's gaze. A tall, lanky guy with tufts of brown hair was smiling over at them. "You look nauseated."

"Actually, that's the sickly glow of love and adoration you're detecting. There's a fine line." Mia swallowed. "Okay, I need backup. I really like this guy."

Bock stepped forward.

"Down, Rambo," Mia said through her teeth to the agent. "Not *that* kind of backup."

"You really like *this* guy?" Sam asked, incredulous. "What about all the ones you've been kissing since school started?"

"When I really like a guy, it means I'm not gonna kiss him," Mia explained, as if it made perfect sense. "Long story short, we went to school together and I've loved Ed since spandex was in. I asked him to meet me tonight, but I never thought he would."

Sam followed Mia's gaze and saw Ed spotting them and giving an enthusiastic wave. Mia gave a shy, totally non-Mia wave back.

"Hey, Samantha, it's really great to meet you," Ed said, walking over to them. "Welcome to Redmond."

"Excuse me," Mia said, quietly backing away and jogging off.

"Wait, Mia, where are you going?" Ed called after her. He turned a confused eye to Sam. "We were supposed to hang out."

Sam watched as Mia blurred into the crowd. Her friend had obviously read Ed's friendly greeting to her as something more.

Now, instead of trying to meet up with James, it looked like Sam had two people to find.

With Bock and Dylan at her side, Sam worked her way through the throngs of people, listening for Mia's voice, trying to spot her bright-colored shirt. Finally, after over an hour of searching, Sam gave up. She walked dejectedly back to Woody House.

What a bust this night had been.

But apparently it wasn't over. Music

was blasting and there were people crowded into her dorm's hall, and as she approached her room, she realized that they were spilling out of her doorway. Most of them were guys, and most of them had a can of beer in their hand.

It seemed as if Mia had decided to throw an impromptu party.

No one noticed as Sam hovered in the doorway.

"Are we supposed to salute or say the Pledge of Allegiance or something?" asked a sleazy-looking girl who had taken Sam's family photo off the hook behind her bed.

Mia grabbed the framed photo. "Hands off the roommate's personals. Only I get to touch them." She picked up a marker and drew horns and mustaches over Sam and her parents.

Sam felt tears sting her eyes as she witnessed the scene in front of her. How could Mia do this to her?

"Dude, I can't believe we're partying, in like, Dorm Room One," said one drunken frat guy.

"Hey, Mia," Mia singsonged to herself.

"Can you introduce me, Mia? What's she like, Mia? Do you get to see her naked, Mia? I'm sick of all things Samantha!"

"I hear you," said the frat guy. "It's gotta be rough." He grinned. "So do you get to see her naked?"

"None of your business," Sam said, and every head in the room swiveled in her direction. "What's going on, Mia?"

"What's going on is, this isn't working out," Mia said, jutting her chin out. "It's too hard. Just because people have to watch your every move doesn't mean I should have to live with it. *I'm* not the President's daughter, remember?"

For once, Sam didn't feel like watching what she said. "Is it that you don't like living with all the attention, Mia . . . or that you don't like living without it?"

"Excuse me?" Mia's eyes shot daggers as people in the room began to file out uncomfortably.

"I think you're used to being the center of things."

"As a matter of fact, I am," Mia retorted.

"But not because my father's the leader of the free world, or so people can tell their parents they sat next to me in the cafeteria, but because that's who I am. Naturally. What you've got going on is genetic lime-light." She crossed her arms. "Now, either you leave or I will."

"You're really acting unreasonable," Sam said, taken aback. "I think we should both just take a minute—"

"I'm not going to count to ten," Mia said hotly. "I'm not going to make a chart. And I will not put it on the itinerary. Right here, right now, let's have this out. Go with your gut, Sam. Don't say what someone told you to say. Just be you . . . whoever that is."

"This from a woman who'll kiss anyone with lips but saves abstinence for the one person she really cares about?" Sam countered as the last person hurried from the room.

"At least I admit I'm messed up," Mia said, flipping her hair back. "You're so desperate to be liked that you'll naively let people use me to get to you and not see what's happening. You'll be nice to people who use me like that?"

"You let that happen regardless of whether I'm around. You make that choice all the time, so don't blame your genetically lit roommate." Sam yanked the photograph of her family away from Mia. "And definitely don't draw on her parents. It's just not nice."

With her defaced photo in her hands, she stormed out of the room.

At first, as the morning light streamed through the windows of Woody House, Sam couldn't figure out where she was. And then it all came back: how she had found refuge in the rec room after her fight with Mia. Apparently she had fallen asleep right where she had sat down. Her back was stiff, her legs were cramped, and her mouth felt dry as cotton. "Ow, ow, ow, ow," she mumbled, rubbing her sore neck.

"You really shouldn't sleep in that position," James said, crouching down in front of her. He wore shorts, a T-shirt, and running shoes, and his skin was glistening. "Bad for the neck."

"I deserve it," Sam croaked. "I'm the devil, see?" She handed the photograph to him. "Artwork compliments of my roommate. I wouldn't want to be friends with me either, reduced security or not. I just need to face it—my life will never be normal."

James leaned in close. "And exactly what's so bad about that?"

"The last time I had privacy, I was in utero," Sam said miserably.

James laughed, but Sam was serious. "Imagine what it's like to never be alone and always feel lonely." She gulped as he looked at her. "You think I'm a silly, spoiled kid, completely devoid of gratitude."

"Actually, I think I completely understand what you go through," James told her.

"You do?"

James nodded. "This one time, back in junior high, I won the class spelling bee." He held up his hands. "Well, needless to say, my life was turned upside down. I couldn't get from point A to B without people watching my every move. I had to deal with the press, the paparazzi." He shook his head. "And the women, oh, the women, Sam. The number of training bras that got left in my locker could have filled the support needs of a small country."

Sam gave him a playful punch in the arm.

"So about last night—" James began.

Sam shrugged. "You're my RA. It's forbidden. I get it."

"It's not just the RA thing—"

"Right, that other thing," Sam said, looking thoughtful. "Most guys have to deal with meeting the dad; my dates have to charm the commander in chief." She held up a finger. "Note to fathers worldwide— best way to keep your daughter from getting any action is to become President."

There was a moment of uncomfortable silence. Then James smiled. "So you were hoping to get some action?"

Sam felt her cheeks flush.

"You need some air?" James asked. "I think I need some air."

"I'll just get changed," Sam said, her heart thumping at the chance to be with James—who cared if he was her RA?—again.

After climbing out the window, scrambling down the fire escape, and taking off in James's car, Sam and James sat in the middle of a San Francisco intersection.

"What's first?" James asked, tapping the wheel with his fingers. "We need a plan."

"First item on the plan: no plans," Sam said firmly. "I propose a whole day of doing whatever, whenever, wherever."

"Sounds like a plan," James agreed. "In a nonplan way, of course."

"In fact, let's follow every green light and see where they take us," Sam said impulsively. James drove along the street, turning this way and that on their green-lit path.

This is awesome! Sam thought as they pulled up to a fabulous grassy park in the middle of the city. A large fountain gurgled, and children were frolicking in the sunshine. Sam and James walked down a shady path to a dock and climbed into a waiting paddleboat.

"My dad used to take me to a spot like this," James said as the boat drifted out into the lake. "He would always say the world was a tough place and you needed total self-reliance to survive it."

"But he must be proud of you," Sam said firmly.

"If he was, he definitely wouldn't say so." James turned toward shore. "How much longer do we have?" he yelled to the boat vendor.

"As long as it takes," the man called back. "One thing I've learned is everything comes back again."

"Let's say you do please your father and you're completely successful and completely self-reliant and you know he's proud of you," Sam said, not about to let James change the subject. "Then what?" She could tell by the look on James's face that he'd never let himself get that far in his dreams.

"It's tough to imagine, right?" she went on, letting her fingers dip into the cool water. "Because then you'd actually have to figure out what *you* want."

"You've thought about this before," James said.

"Every day of my life," Sam admitted.

A street carnival had been set up along one of the city piers, and after a day of boating, snacking, and roaming, Sam and James found themselves swept up in a river of fairgoers. The lights of the rides, the carnival barkers trying to lure in new players, the smell of cotton candy, and the masses of people—it was like heaven to Sam. So when James pulled her into an empty space between game booths, she wasn't ready for a break.

"Let's get back in there!" she told him, her eyes wild with excitement. She didn't want it to end.

"Wait a minute," James cautioned, laughing. "Catch your breath."

"Nobody was looking at me or making

room for me," Sam said, astonished. "Nobody was warned to keep their distance. It was amazing!" She squeezed James's hand—the hand that had been holding hers for the past ten minutes. "How do you do that?"

"Do what?"

Sam exhaled. "When I'm with you, I'm just . . . me. Sam. Not the First Daughter. I really like it."

James licked his lips. "Sam. You're—"

"So are you," Sam blurted out before he could finish.

He laughed, giving her hand a tug. "All right, then. Let's get in there. You lead."

They blended back into the crowd, taking in the various sights, until they came upon a booth selling Chinese food. A tiny Asian woman operated the stand.

"May I have two, please?" Sam asked in perfect Mandarin, pointing to two giant pieces of honey-cured pork.

"One for you and one for your boyfriend," the woman said in her native tongue, giving James the once-over.

Sam quickly glanced at him to see if he

had understood. But of course he hadn't. He was too busy looking dumbfounded that she could even speak Chinese.

"I wish," Sam said conspiratorially to the woman, taking the pork and handing one to James. "You must try this," she insisted. "Think of it as a giant beef jerky."

She took a huge bite. So did James.

"So?" she prompted. "Do you love it?"

James winced. "This is . . . awful! I don't know what impresses me more: that you like this, or that you speak Chinese."

From there they moved on to a water-pistol booth. Sam raced to an available water gun. Then James pulled her back.

"Hey, Your Highness—line's back here," he said, leading her by the arm to the end of the line, apologizing to the people who gave them dirty looks.

Sam felt like an idiot. But she wasn't used to waiting in line. She never even gave it a thought.

"See, a line is something people form when they need to take turns," James said slowly, as if she were a child.

"Interesting," Sam said, putting her

fingers on her chin. "Tell me more about these 'people' you speak of."

When at last it was their turn, Sam was prepared to whip James's butt.

Except he whipped hers.

"You beat me," Sam said with a sigh, giving the counter a slap.

"No . . . I kicked your butt," James amended.

"Thank you," Sam said, and she really meant it. "Most people let me win." It was nice to be treated like a real person for once, lines and all.

"You never have to worry about that with me," he told her.

"Good." Sam pointed to the water pistol. "Now show me what to do." She pulled him into place behind her, putting his hands over hers to secure the pistol. As they stood together, James's fingers brushed against the charm bracelet on her wrist.

"My dad gave it to me," Sam explained, turning to face him. "One charm for every new country, every continent, every election won. Something for all our trips together."

For a moment Sam thought James was going to kiss her. She wanted him to kiss her.

But instead, James motioned her to a souvenir booth, one that turned a coin into a memento. James placed a penny in the slot, and a few seconds later the machine popped out a flattened souvenir.

"For your bracelet," James said, dropping it into Sam's open palm. "Just the first of all the trips you're gonna take on your own."

Sam's fingers curled around the penny. It was such an incredibly sweet thing to do.

She wished she had the courage to tell him something, though.

A kiss would have been the best souvenir of all.

"So, this is my stop," Sam said as they walked down the dorm hall to her room. After all the closeness they had shared, it felt weird to suddenly feel so uncomfortable.

"That's your room," James agreed.

"Yeah, I like it. It's a nice room."

"Spacious for a double."

"That's exactly what I said to Mia."

"Well, that was fun," James and Sam said in unison.

James coughed. "I guess I should—"

"Me too," Sam said hastily.

"Good night, then, Samantha."

"Good night, James."

She tried not to let it bother her that James turned and walked quickly down the hall to his room. But it did bother her. It bothered her a lot. She stopped trying to get the key in its lock and hurried down the hall after him. He had just let himself in when she skidded to a stop in front of him, her heart in her throat.

Before she knew what she was doing, she had pulled him into her arms and was kissing him with all her heart.

A few seconds later, Sam walked back to her room, unable to stop smiling. She had kissed him! And better yet, he had kissed her back.

And then some.

"I know you're mad at me now, but I kissed him and that takes precedence, right?" Sam blurted out as she burst into her room.

Mia and some guy were making out on Mia's bed. "Oh, sorry, I'll just—"

"No, Sam, stay," Mia said.

"Really?"

"Yeah, really?" the guy asked Mia, looking hurt.

"I need to hang out with my roommate tonight," she told him, gently shoving him off the bed. "You should go." When he had left, she gave Sam a hug.

"I know I'm hard to live with," Sam said, hugging her back. "I know you didn't want to be my roommate."

"Stop," Mia said. "Come with me, Sam." She pulled Sam down the hallway to a door decorated with little trombone decals.

The door opened. A giggling redhead stood staring at them. She clapped a hand to her mouth. "I can't believe it!" she squealed, gawking at Sam. "It's really you. Coming to my room!"

"Sam, allow me to introduce our dorm-mate," Mia said. "This is Linda, of Paterson, New Jersey. She plays the trombone." Then she leaned over and whispered, "And my original roommate."

Of course. "Linda of Paterson, plays trombone." Sam held out her hand. "Nice to meet you."

Linda stepped back. "Don't move!" In a burst of enthusiasm, she grabbed her trombone and belted out an impromptu "Hail to the Chief."

Sam stifled a laugh. "Wow."

"I know, wow, right?" Mia said. "Linda practices four hours a day—get this—in her room. Isn't that fantastic?"

"Bulletproof glass is looking pretty good right now, huh?" Sam whispered to Mia.

"It's looking great, actually," Mia said, beaming.

chapter**nine**

The next day, Sam had a plan. A big plan. A plan guaranteed to shock, surprise, and totally thrill her friends—after giving them momentary heart attacks. That morning, she had spoken to Liz. Everything was set. She had arranged for Bock and Dylan to accompany Mia and James by car to the airport. When their small motorcade pulled up on the runway where Sam stood and Mia and James got out, confused expressions on their faces, Sam waved.

"Anybody up for a study break?" Sam quipped.

"What is going on?" Mia asked, her eyes glued to the plane behind Sam. Which happened to be Air Force One.

Sam's eyes shone with glee. "You're being kidnapped."

As they boarded the plane, Mia was freaking out. "I can't believe I'm on Air Force One. Now, this is a road trip!"

Sam had flown on Air Force One so many times that it had lost a bit of its luster to her. But seeing a civilian—especially a friend—board for the first time was always exciting.

"You guys have put up with a lot from me," Sam told them. "I just wanted to do something special for you."

One of the stewards led the way down the aisle.

"And who might you be?" Mia asked, giving him an appreciative once-over.

"This is Charles," Sam cut in with a smile. She'd never given it much thought, but the steward was pretty cute. "He's here to assist you with anything you may want."

"You mean serve my every whim?" Mia

asked, immediately warming to the notion. "My every whim?"

Charles nodded. "Absolutely."

Mia gave him a devilish wink. "Because I can be whimsical."

Sam and her friends continued through the plane to the communication center. James was looking around in awe, while Mia couldn't keep her eyes off Charles.

"Nice equipment!"

"Excuse me?" Charles said.

"The computers," Mia added. Then she motioned over his shoulder. "Can you hack into virtually any computer in the world?"

"Yes," Charles said.

"Good, so you can raise my limit on my Neiman's account," Mia said loftily. "A couple more zeroes would be good."

Charles swept his arm across the room. "Just Neiman's? What about Saks? Barneys?"

Sam hoped he was only kidding. She led her friends into one of the plane's plush seating areas, where several comfortable chairs were arranged along with basins of bubbling water. A smiling woman was waiting for them. Beside her on a low table were fluffy white towels, pumice stones, lotions, and a variety of colorful nail polishes.

"Marjorie is here to help us get ready, starting with manicures and pedicures," Sam explained happily. "Then, when we land, we'll find something to wear." She pointed to the two plasma TVs. On one was a basketball game. On the other, a baseball game. "James, every game you can imagine is stacked in there—my dad's private collection." Sam took in her friends' stunned expressions. "I—I hope this isn't too much."

In response, Mia plopped into a chair and dunked her fingers into a bowl of water. James sat down a bit more slowly in a recliner and began flipping through TV channels.

"Um, where are we going?" he asked, staring up at Sam.

Her heart flip-flopped at the realization that he was really here—and she had really pulled this off. "It's a surprise."

Just then Charles came down the aisle,

pushing a cart full of the most incredibly delicious desserts imaginable. Sam should know—she had sampled them many times.

Mia sighed. "Is this a great country or what?"

"May I get you something to eat, Ms. Thompson?"

Several hours later, as the plane flew over Washington, D.C., and the breathtaking vista of the city came into view, Sam, James, and Mia were sitting together, gazing out the windows.

"Mia, James," Sam said, sweeping her arms in a grand gesture. "Welcome to your nation's capital."

She couldn't wait for them to see what she had planned. A limo would be waiting at the airport to take them to their first stop: a personal fitting for evening gowns handled by none other than Vera Wang herself. Then James would be off to be outfitted in a tux for tonight's huge fund-raising event downtown.

That sight alone would be worth the flight.

Outside the Ritz-Carlton, paparazzi, their cameras flashing, were calling out the names of the guests. Crowds were held back by velvet ropes and police barricades. A small group of protesters held signs.

Sam looked anxiously out the window. She hadn't seen James since he had left to get his tux. As they pulled up to the gold-trimmed steps of the hotel, she beamed. There he was, waiting at the end of the red carpet. He looked nervous.

He looked hot.

Mia's face was flushed with excitement as she stepped out of the car first, wearing a beautiful new Vera Wang gown. She mugged for the brightly flashing cameras.

Taking a deep breath, Sam emerged from the car. She felt like a princess in her pale pink one-of-a-kind Vera Wang dress. Whisper-thin spaghetti straps held the dress up, and a long ribbon was wrapped around her waist and tied in a bow. The full skirt skimmed the carpet, barely grazing the toes of her elegant pumps. Her hair was pulled back into a chignon, and diamonds dangled from her ears.

"Sorry we're late," she said as she glided toward James.

He swallowed. "I'm not."

Sam gave his tux an admiring look. "And I was right."

She slid her gloved hand into the crook of his arm and up the steps they went.

Everything in the grand hotel ballroom was decorated in red, white, and blue— from the table linens and huge floral center-pieces to the artfully arranged streamers and patriotic balloon bouquets that filled every vacant spot. Mackenzie supporters were everywhere. A small orchestra played and tuxedo-clad waiters milled about with trays of wineglasses and hors d'oeuvres.

Sam guided her friends toward the

presidential receiving line, where her parents stood greeting their guests.

Mia stepped forward first. "Mr. and Mrs. President, Mia Thompson . . . the one in the thong?" she said by way of introduction.

The President smiled. "Of course, Mia. Lovely to meet you."

Sam tugged on James's arm. He looked quite pale. "Dad, this is James, my RA. And my—" She hesitated, not sure what she should say.

James extended his hand. "It's a pleasure to meet you, Mr. President."

Her father gave his hand a firm shake. "And you, James."

"And my mother," Sam added eagerly.

"Mrs. Mackenzie," James said. "You're even lovelier in person."

Her mother smiled. "Please. Call me Melanie."

As usual, other guests soon occupied her parents. But for once Sam didn't mind. She beamed as James pulled her close. "Can we go talk somewhere?" he asked.

Instead, she took his arm and led him over to the dance floor. "Place your right hand—"

"What are you—"

"I'm dancing with you," Sam said simply.

James looked around the ballroom. "But no one else is dancing," he pointed out.

"And isn't it a shame?" She placed his hand on her waist. "Here."

He sighed. "I need a minute alone—"

"And I need you to take my left hand," Sam insisted. They began to dance, with Sam leading.

"We shouldn't—we can't do this," James protested weakly.

"Why not?" Sam said, gazing up at him. "It's a free country. I don't care what he says. Call out the National Guard. Nothing is stopping me from dancing with you tonight. Tonight I'm making my own itinerary, and it happens to feel great." She was just about to snuggle her head against his chest when Liz Pappas walked up.

"Go away," Sam ordered, turning her

head. Liz did an immediate about-face and retreated.

"See that?" Sam smiled. "I'm going to spin now." She twirled out in a circle and spun back in.

"Now hold me," she told James. "Hold me close."

For a moment, James hesitated. Then he too did exactly what she had asked.

Soon the dance floor filled up, and the two of them danced to song after song. Everyone had stopped to hear Sam's father give some brief welcoming remarks, and then he took to the floor with Sam's mother.

Mia swirled by with a handsome dark-haired guy. "Is Vanuatu really a country?" she whispered as she passed Sam. "Because this guy says he's ambassador of it."

Sam giggled and gave Mia a thumbs-up.

"Now, where were we?" Sam said, looking up at James and feeling like more of a princess than ever.

When the gala ended, Sam and her friends went to join the President and First Lady—and their Secret Service detail—outside the hotel. Hordes of photographers still jockeyed for position, and protesters continued to chant anti-Mackenzie slogans and wave their signs.

"Did you have fun, Mia?" Sam's mother asked as if they were the only ones present.

"You mean, with the free dress, the all-you-can-eat caviar, and a few very fine diplomats?" Mia grinned. "On the fun meter, I'd give it a nine. Get me on your next invite list, you might get the ten."

Everyone laughed, the President hardest of all.

As Sam and James made their way through the crowd, reporters began peppering her with questions.

"What do you think of your father's domestic policy, Samantha?" one reporter with an obvious ax to grind shouted at her. "Does your education suffer for it?"

Sam felt flustered at the unusually personal attack. "I—I feel my father's administration gives a great deal of attention to our domestic policy." She caught the eye of one of the protesters, and it rattled her. "His, uh, his college-tuition tax credit initiative, for example. I—"

"You know he's a fraud!" shouted a protester. "Your dad's a fraud!"

James stepped in, looking angry. "Hey, back off, man."

Suddenly, there was a squeal of tires. Everyone turned to see a car, spinning out of control, on a collision course with the President's motorcade.

People began diving for cover, surging forward and pushing past the barricades.

Sam gasped as the car smashed into one of the limos in the motorcade, the horrifying sounds of crunching steel and spraying glass shattering the evening calm. Then she was shoved away from James, getting caught in the panicked crowd.

"Hey!" she cried as photographers and reporters angling to get a shot of the accident scene knocked her to the ground.

Then James was there, rescuing her. He

threw Sam across his shoulder like a rag doll and got them out of there. She felt as if she were in a dream as he carried her back into the hotel through the lobby.

"Where's Mia?" Sam asked, concerned, trying to look back out at the accident scene. "James, put me down!"

"Bock will take care of Mia," he said, never slowing his stride. He carried her, still slung over his shoulder, across the lobby and into a stairwell. Seconds later they were in the hotel's garage.

Sam blinked as a Secret Service Suburban pulled up. *But how did James know to bring me here?* she thought, bewildered.

A car door opened and he put her in the backseat.

And then he spoke into his sleeve. "Lucky Charm secure."

Sam stared dumbfounded at James. "James?" she whispered, feeling as if her entire world had ground to a halt. James Lamson, her RA, her new boyfriend . . . was Secret Service? It couldn't be.

It had to be.

He looked back at her wordlessly as he slammed the Suburban's door shut.

The car began to move. And amid the swirling lights and the chaotic scene, Sam stared out the window, pressing her crestfallen face to the glass. James grew smaller and smaller as they drove away. And when the car turned the corner, he was gone.

chapter**ten**

Back at the White House, Sam was furious.

Her father leaned forward in his chair. "Samantha, honey, I'm—"

"Don't," Sam said, cutting him off. "There's nothing you can say." She turned to look at Bock, standing behind her. "Did you know? Bock?"

His nervous silence was all the answer she needed. "Was there anybody who didn't know except for me?" she asked angrily. "Of course not, I'm the fool."

The President sat back. "Don't you understand that every day I get half a dozen threats against you? As your father, I could never live with myself if anything happened. And as your President, I know this country cannot afford to have you harmed. What could I do, Samantha? What choice did I have?"

"You had the choice to be honest with me," Sam choked out. "You had the choice not to lie—as my father and as the President."

"I know you thought he was your friend," her father said, the remark cutting her to the core. *Friend?* "If you'd prefer, we could have James replaced."

She buried her head in her hands. How could she prefer that? "Will he lose his job?" she asked.

"He'll be transferred off First Family detail, but he'll still have a position," her father told her.

"But not the right position."

"He's in line to protect me now," her father said matter-of-factly. "And yes, that is where most agents want to end up."

Sam took a long, deep breath. No matter how she felt, she couldn't make a choice that would hurt James. None of this was his fault. "He can stay."

"I really hope you come to understand this one day," her father said, crossing the room and sitting down beside her.

"I already do," Sam said quietly. "That's what's so disappointing."

"I thought I'd finally found someone who really liked me . . . just for me," Sam said, staring up at the ceiling. She and Mia lay side by side on Sam's bed at the White House.

"And how do you know his feelings for you weren't real?" Mia asked.

Sam sighed, wondering where James was, what was happening to him. "He was just doing his job."

Mia snorted. "That's crap. He wanted you. Watch. Go on like nothing happened." Her eyebrows drew together. "Better yet, date somebody. There's nothing a man wants more than something he can't have."

It was a quiet morning in the Rose Garden as Sam stood with her packed bags at her feet. She gave her mother a hug.

"Did you say goodbye to your father?" her mother asked her.

Sam gave her mom an incredulous look. Was she kidding? Why would she say goodbye to someone she was furious with?

Her mother frowned, then motioned her to move off to the side, away from the few staff members who had assembled to help. "A little history lesson, Sam—just hear me out. In 1981, James's father took a bullet for Reagan. And in 1963, if they had listened to James's grandfather, Kennedy would never have been riding in an open convertible that day."

"He mentioned the family business," Sam muttered. "He just left out the part about the Kevlar vests."

"He's one of the best agents to come along in years, Sam," her mother said quietly.

"And?"

"And your father wanted you to have the best," her mother answered. "He's always watching over you."

Sam fiddled with her charm bracelet. "Yeah," she said after a few seconds of silence. "I know."

When Sam returned to college, everything had changed. James didn't have to pretend that he was an RA, a regular old student just like everyone else. Now he wore a suit, a tie, and uncomfortable-looking shoes and fell right into step with Bock and Dylan.

"I just wanted to thank you," James said, coming up beside her in the library stacks as she pretended to look for a book. He cleared his throat and lowered his voice. "I crossed a line and you could have had me fired for that. I just wanted you to know

I appreciate it. And I'm really sorry I had to deceive you."

Sam gave him a civil smile. "Hey, we're all just living Pinocchios, right?"

"Right," James said as she walked away.

Later that day, Sam walked over to the Student Health and Wellness Center. *Time to make James really squirm,* she thought with grim determination as she took a seat in the waiting room with James and Bock.

"Ms. Mackenzie?" the receptionist called out after a few moments.

"I'm here for my birth control appointment," Sam said loudly. A few students raised their eyebrows. James's face was blank.

Once inside the examination room, she spoke frankly to the nurse-practitioner. "So if you could just give me as many samples as possible, that would be great."

The woman looked at her askance.

"I mean, it's not for me," she added hastily. "I'm trying to make this guy jealous. Seriously. I just want him to think that maybe, you know, there's a lot of action going on."

The dubious woman put a handful of condoms into a bag for her.

"More action," Sam said.

The woman added a few more.

Sam shook her head. "No . . . more like spring-break-in-Daytona kind of action."

When she left the center, Sam had a gigantic bag of birth control supplies slung over her shoulder.

Take that, James Lamson, she thought smugly as the agents trailed behind her. *Better yet, maybe I'll ask him to carry it!*

Tonight's Halloween party is going to be something, Sam thought as she got dressed in her dorm room. She'd already forced James to tag along on a date with an extremely hot frat guy, and this would be the final touch in her make-James-sickeningly-jealous plan. She put on a pair of super-short Daisy Duke shorts and adjusted the tiny strips of material that served as a halter. Then she pulled on a platinum blond wig that grazed her hips and topped it with a fuzzy pink cowboy hat. "There," she said, with a satisfied smile. She slipped on a pair of dangerously high Lucite platform heels and struck a sexy pose for Mia.

Otherwise known as Kid Rock. Mia wore a wife beater, jeans, and a black bowler hat. Her arms were covered with scary-looking temporary tattoos, and her hair was stuffed under a stringy blond wig.

Mia held up a full bottle of Jack Daniel's. "We sure don't look like your parents," she said, naming what had been the original idea for their costumes.

And that was the entire point.

Arm in arm, they strode out of Woody House and crossed the campus, heading toward one of the more popular campus bars. All around them, people did double takes.

"Okay, now I'm beginning to regret the outfit choice," Sam said under her breath as she wobbled across the grass. Bock and James were several feet behind them. "Who was I kidding? I can't pull this off." She motioned with her eyes behind them. "Is it even working?"

Mia gave a slight nod. "You got yourself into this, and you're going to follow through."

"You're right." Sam spoke more loudly. "Besides, I have a date expecting me." She lowered her voice. "What's his name again?"

"Frank."

The party at the bar was in full swing when they arrived. And after a few drinks, Sam was in full swing too.

"To speak frankly, Frank, the life of a college student is growing on me by the minute," she told the frat guy she'd had dinner with a few days before. Her body buzzed from the liquor. "Furthermore, you are growing on me by the minute."

Frank leered at her. "Thanks. You too."

Sam flagged down a passing patron. "Hey, you, is my date a babe or what?"

Out of the corner of her eye, she could

see that James was worried. Very worried. He said something into his headset, his forehead creased.

Things were going extremely well.

I should have let loose like this a long time ago, Sam thought as music blasted even more loudly through the jammed bar. She downed another shot, then shimmied over to the nearby bar and climbed onto it.

"Sam! Sam! Sam!" the crowd chanted, going nuts. Frank climbed up to join her. They began to dance, and Sam did moves she'd only seen on MTV Spring Break specials. People began taking pictures, and Sam posed provocatively as Frank gave her halter top strings a tug. *Screw Washington! Screw James!* Frank slapped her butt. *Screw—*

Wham! She stumbled backward as James punched Frank squarely in the jaw. And in a reenactment of the fund-raising chaos, he stepped forward, slung Sam over his shoulder, and strode out the barroom door.

Sam struggled to free herself as he carried her down the street. "I'm not four years old, James. Put me down!" She blinked rapidly, her head spinning slightly. "I can walk."

James kept moving. "The thing is, you can't. Let me help you, Samantha."

"Why should I?" she asked, feeling tears rush to her eyes. "Why should I trust you, James? You lied to me, you made me like you. . . . Why are you doing this?"

"Because you're out of control."

"No, I meant this job." Sam squirmed some more. "I saw your file, mister. You dropped out of training one time, took a personal leave another."

"This isn't the time—"

"Why are you a Secret Service agent?" Sam persisted, struggling to get free.

James tightened his grip. "Honestly, right now I'm just trying to get through this and do my job, which, by the way, you are making very difficult. What are you doing, Sam? This isn't you."

Just like that, Sam gave up the fight. "This *is* me, James. Me without you."

By the time they got back to Woody

House, Sam was half asleep. She let herself slump in James's arms as he unlocked the door to her room, laid her down on her bed, and gently kissed her forehead.

"What are you doing?" Sam demanded, her eyes flicking open.

James looked startled. "I was just saying good night."

She sat up, her face serious. "What is this? Some kind of game to you?" She swallowed. "You don't have to pretend anymore."

"You're an amazing girl—" he began awkwardly.

"Don't!" Sam blurted out. "No more lies."

James sighed and his shoulders suddenly sagged. "What could I have given you, Sam? I don't have anything to offer—you're the President's daughter, for God's sake."

"I've spent almost my whole life with people smiling at me, laughing at my jokes," Sam said quietly. "And right now, I don't know if any of that was true. Maybe it was all some kind of act." She hesitated, then voiced her biggest fear. "What if I weren't the First Daughter, James? Would they still laugh? If things were different? If I were just like everyone else, how would you feel about me then?"

"But things aren't different," James said doggedly.

"But if they were," Sam persisted. "You at least owe me this. Forget politics. Forget image. Forget everything but who I am right now in here." She pointed to her heart. "If things were different."

James kept his eyes on hers. "If things were different, I'd still follow you around all the time. Because I wanted to . . . not because I had to."

She trembled as he leaned forward and kissed her tenderly on the mouth. Then he left.

And she crumbled.

Sam would be forever grateful to Mia, she decided as she lay nearly comatose in

141

bed, the biggest hangover in the world pounding her head. Mia had been fielding phone calls all morning—and apparently she'd also told James off but good last night when he'd slunk out of her room.

"She's not here," Mia said robotically, picking up the ringing phone.

"Hello, you have reached Moviefone," she said at the next series of rings. "If you know the name of your movie . . ."

"I'm sorry about all the calls," Sam mumbled, raising a clammy hand to her forehead.

"Don't worry about that," Mia said. "You know, you are a really photogenic young lady. I would kill for your ass." She pointed to the cover of *The New York Post*. There, for all the world to see, was a photo of Sam dirty dancing on the bar, accompanied by the headline SAM GONE WILD! FIRST LAP DANCE!

Sam shuddered, then looked out the window at the hordes of press camped out below. She pulled the covers over her head as the phone rang once more.

"Take a number, buddy," Mia said. "Oh! Hey, Liz."

Sam shot up and took the phone.

"Sam, your father is extremely disappointed," Liz said. "Is it true?"

"It was just one night, Liz," Sam said weakly, rubbing her throbbing temples. "One very bad night."

"I'm not talking about your night. I'm talking about your boyfriend."

"What are you talking about?" Sam asked, confused. "Just let me talk to him." It was pointless to have this conversation with Liz when what she really needed to do was discuss it with her father.

"Uh, he's unavailàble right now," Liz said, her uncertainty a dead giveaway that she was lying. Then Sam heard a whoosh of static as the phone changed hands.

"I can't talk to you right now, Samantha!" her father barked into the phone. "You went too far." And then he hung up.

Sam was still clutching the phone when Mia gasped from where she stood by their door. "Sam!" She held up a copy of *The*

National Enquirer that had been slipped under the door. SAM SECRETLY SERVICED! screamed the headline, accompanied by a photograph that looked suspiciously like the one taken by the old woman from the pizza parlor.

She shot out of bed, got dressed, brushed her hair and her teeth, and splashed some cold water on her face. Then she slowly opened her door. To her relief, James was at his post.

"James?" she said tentatively.

He turned. *Who the heck are you?* she thought, distressed to see a much older stranger's face. "Who are you? Where is James?"

"I'm Agent Dreyer, ma'am. Mr. Lamson is no longer on this detail."

She forced herself to walk down the hall, past the TV lounge. A group of students were watching CNN. "The White House had no comment regarding a jealous brawl in which Samantha Mackenzie was involved, nor her alleged relationship with one of her Secret Service agents," stated the news anchor.

This was the last straw. Sam fled to her room and slammed the door in Agent Dreyer's face.

A face that could never replace James Lamson's.

Sam wanted to forget about James. But she couldn't seem to, no matter how hard she tried. Talking with Mia, studying, listening to CDs, going online—nothing worked. In a last-ditch effort, she tried jogging. She pushed her body to the limit, running well beyond the distances she covered as part of her regular exercise routine.

Of course, she couldn't jog alone. Bock and Dylan jogged right behind her, and a government-issue car trailed them as well.

But it was no use. Without warning, Sam stopped, resting her hands on her bare knees and sobbing in the middle of the street. *What am I supposed to do? Forget that I met one person who really understands me?*

And as her security entourage watched

her cry from their objective positions on the side, Sam had never felt more alone.

When she finally stumbled back into her room, she gasped. Her mother was sitting on her bed.

"Mom! What are you doing here?"

"The question on my mind is what have you been doing here, Samantha?"

Sam ran over and hugged her, hanging her head.

"There's been a three-point drop because of your table dance."

That was election-speak for the polls. "Was I that bad?" Sam attempted to joke.

Her mother would have none of it. "You've got to know we're in the race of our lives," she said quietly. "The voters expect more of us. We were elected to set an example. That's the life we've chosen."

"But I didn't choose anything, Mom," Sam said. "And I didn't run for anything. Nobody elected me, remember?"

"Like it or not, chosen or not, you are the daughter of the President of the United States," her mother said with conviction.

"You are not allowed to make the same mistakes as a regular teenager. You're a Mackenzie. Your father and I need you. We need to be the First Family now."

The realization of what her mother was getting at hit her. "You want me to leave school," Sam said dully.

"Margaret Thatcher once said, 'If you want anything said, ask a man. If you want anything done, ask a woman.' We have to get your father the presidency. It's his time now."

"You're asking me to join the campaign," Sam said, putting her thoughts into words.

Her mother gave a small smile. "I'm not just asking."

Sam went to the rest of her classes that day, more of a zombie than a real student. She barely paid attention to anything her professors said.

"Anyone?" her English professor was

asking. "At the end of the day, the prince is—"

"Just a prince," Sam spoke up, tearing her attention away from the window.

"Go on," her professor encouraged, clearly glad to have a response from somebody.

"It didn't matter how much he trusted or gave of himself or his possessions, at the end of the day, the prince is, and will always be, a prince. He will always be different." And with that, Sam collected her books, slung them into her backpack, and walked out of the classroom.

"This is a terrible idea," Mia said, fuming, as Sam tossed her things into her suitcases.

"Then we'll have to agree to disagree," Sam said, not slowing her pace.

"People never stick things out," Mia muttered. "They always leave."

Sam halted, a sweater in her hands. "I'm not leaving *you*, Mia."

Mia grabbed Sam's bag and threw it on

the floor. "You have a responsibility to stay. A responsibility to yourself and to the people who look to you to have some grace under pressure. This isn't you, Sam."

"And forgive me if I'm not exactly sure who that is for one minute," Sam said, feeling as if she was going to cry. "Can't I just, for once, not know what to do, who to be, or where to go? Would that be okay? All I know right now is that my family needs me."

"What about what *you* need?" Mia pressed.

"That's just it, Mia—they're the same thing."

"Well, what about crying?" Mia said, crossing her arms. "Is that okay? I won't tell if you don't."

Sam sniffed. "I don't have time for that." She kept packing.

"I was promised a roommate, remember?" Mia asked, wrapping her arms around herself. "Don't leave, Sam."

Sam couldn't take it any longer. She put down her things and gave Mia a hug.

But circumstances couldn't change.

In one hour her bags would be loaded into the presidential limo, and with Sam and her mother seated inside, the motorcade would leave campus. Tonight she would be sleeping in the White House, and most likely she would scurry down the hallway, unseen, to the kitchen, where, if she was lucky, she could eat a piece of delicious chocolate cake alone, in the dark.

That was just how things worked when you were a Mackenzie.

Transcript from the conversation of Agent James Lamson and his superior, Agent Bill Peters, regarding his actions concerning his assignment, Samantha Mackenzie.

Agent Peters: We're here to discuss the proposed disciplinary action. James Lamson, your record is exceptional, up to now. Looking at this report, I have my doubts about your ability to continue as an agent.

Agent Lamson: I understand.

Agent Peters: Certainly, continuing to work with the protectee is out of the question.

Agent Lamson: Of course.

Agent Peters: Please tell this panel why we should allow you to continue as an agent.

Agent Lamson: My father was an agent. And my grandfather before him.

Agent Peters: They're not the ones under review here. You are. And if you had a different father or grandfather, you wouldn't have this opportunity.

Agent Lamson: I appreciate your time.

Agent Peters: Is it true you became personally involved with Samantha Mackenzie?

Agent Lamson: I did.

Agent Peters: Do you have anything to say to defend your actions?

Agent Lamson: You trained me to expect the unexpected. Well, that's what happened. The person I was protecting turned out to be the most amazing woman, who's going to give something extraordinary to the world one day. And I tried not to feel anything, to keep my distance, but I fell deeper and deeper. I can see now that it impaired my ability to function as an agent. For that, I'm sorry. But the further I crossed the line, the further I went, the more I realized I would never allow her to be put in harm's way. And if having those feelings means losing my job, then it's a loss I'm prepared to take. As a little kid, I always dreamed of standing on the sidelines of history protecting others. Maybe even the President himself. Well, I got to protect this remarkable woman. And I'm not sure what I gave her, but there is one thing I now know I can give her. And it's the one thing I do well—I keep people safe. Because that's what I do—that's who I am. I keep people safe.

Agent Peters: You and I know that mistakes in our line of work could mean someone's life. I'm sorry. You'll be on probation indefinitely. And you should start to think about other alternatives.

Agent Lamson: I understand. Thank you.

[Agent Lamson departed the room.]

chapter**eleven**

Sam stared out into a sea of red, white, and blue balloons as a Detroit high school band played the familiar patriotic anthem.

"We're in great shape, Motor City!" the President called out, waving to the crowd. Sam managed a small smile, but the thought of repeating this scene later that day in Cleveland and then Pittsburgh was more than she could bear.

Backstage later that night at a Pittsburgh fund-raiser, Sam stood quietly in the corner, watching as her father, his staff, and her mother discussed last-minute strategy.

She played absently with her charm bracelet, and when her fingers came to the flattened penny James had given her at the street carnival, the memory of that day came rushing back.

Her father stood up and walked over to her. His lips were drawn together in a grim line. "Look, you're unhappy. I get it. But if you're gonna be here, be here. There's a lot at stake. I need you to be a grown-up now."

"Obviously I understand what's at stake," Sam told him, anger welling up inside her. "I've been standing by your side with Mom for years. And I am still here. But if you want me to be a grown-up, then you have to let me."

And with that, she did what no one else ever dared to do. She turned her back on the President and walked away.

Back at the White House the next day, Sam shivered as she waited outside in the cold. Snow had begun to fall, and the great front lawn of the White House was dusted with white. But when she saw Mia's familiar face pop out of the sedan, her heart warmed.

"I won't lie to you, Sam," Mia said as she walked toward her. "It was tough flying commercial. But when my roommate calls, I'm there. Remember, I'm up for anything."

"I've missed you, Mia," Sam said, hugging her friend. Mia's being there for moral support was the best gift anyone could have given her.

Well, almost the best.

"The good news is, you finally got what you wished for," Mia said.

"What's that?"

"A good old-fashioned broken heart." Mia gave her hand a squeeze. "One of the most normal experiences a gal can have."

"Our biggest successes are in foreign policy," her mother said the next day as they hit the campaign trail once more. "*That's* what we emphasize."

Sam stared off into space. It seemed as if she had spent her entire life backstage on the campaign trail, listening to speech-writers and policy advisors and drinking too many cups of lukewarm coffee.

"With all due respect, not when we've just taken direct hits on the domestic agenda and it's the last push before the election," the press secretary said, waving a handful of papers in the air.

"Sam, what do you think?" the President called over to her.

Startled, Sam turned to her father. "What?"

"I'd like your opinion," the President told her as everyone waited. "I value your opinion, Sam."

"I don't really have an opinion," she said, shrugging. *Not one that he'd want to hear, at least.*

Her father smiled. "Somehow, I seriously doubt that."

Well, if he wanted the truth, she could give him that. "Okay, then, I'm not sure what could be more important than, well, home."

"Thank you, Sam," her father said, rising to his feet. He nodded to the stage manager and prepared to make his entrance.

"Ladies and gentlemen," said the announcer, "the First Family." And Sam walked out with her parents, waving to the crowd and flashing a broad smile.

Only she knew that it was a big fat fraud.

Inside the Democratic National Headquarters in Washington, D.C., a deluge of ticker tape and red, white, and blue balloons fell from the ceilings. Footage of fireworks played on two huge monitors that flanked the stage. The crowd was going wild.

The President hugged the First Lady. "We did it, Mel," he said, beaming.

"We did, John," she said, beaming back.

The crowd was on their feet, cheering and clapping wildly.

Sam smiled. She was truly happy for her parents. But knowing that she was in for four more years of scrutiny made it a bit hard to accept.

A few nights later, when some of the hoopla had died down, Sam was reading in her room. There was a knock on the door, and then it opened. Her father stood there, carrying a plate with a piece of cake, and an old teacup filled with hot chocolate.

"I thought you might need a snack," he said, indicating the plate. "I made your favorite."

Sam's eyebrows rose.

"Okay, I had your favorite made," he amended, sitting down beside her.

"Thanks," she said, accepting it. She took a bite. "Mmm, this is good. Dad, I need you to make sure that James is okay." She'd wanted to mention James for days, but somehow it never seemed like the right time.

Her father was silent for a moment. "He's a good agent, Sam. He should work a good detail. I'll take care of him."

"Thank you, Dad," Sam said.

He got up to leave, then stopped by the door. "Did you love him?"

"I loved who I got to be with him," Sam said truthfully. She'd had a lot of time to think about it. "And even though I didn't do anything that was so amazing . . . for me, it was. I felt like I knew myself for the first time." She bit her lip. "But, yeah, him too."

"That's what I thought," her father said.

The Inaugural Ball was the event of the year, and Sam was dressed to kill in another custom-made Vera Wang gown. She stood alongside her mother as her father addressed the crowd. To her surprise, his speech wasn't composed of a list of thank-yous or his thoughts on all the important issues of the day. It was about . . . her.

"Once upon a time, there was a little girl just like any other little girl," he began. "She liked ballet. She loved to host tea parties. And she kept collections of many beautiful things, always sharing them with her friends. Like many young girls, this one experienced a few growing pains."

Sam blushed, remembering her gawky twelve-year-old self. "And as is often the case, she felt that the whole world was watching." Which, in her case, they had been. "But eventually, she muddled through, and as she blossomed, she became more comfortable in her own skin. Like any normal teenager, she enjoyed parties and pizza, and like her peers, she often felt as if her every move was scrutinized."

Her father cleared his throat. "But with maturity, she was able to look outside herself and appreciate the wisdom of her elders."

The crowd smiled appreciatively.

"In short, she grew up happily, with the love of a mother and a father who she thought were the center of the world in an old white house they called home. And that little girl who grew up in that white house she called home was as different as different can be. But not because she lived in a famous mansion or knew important people, but because of who she had become."

Sam, touched, smiled and reached to hold her mother's hand.

"Recently, this very wise young woman pointed out the importance of home, and over the next four years, this administration will find its way back . . . starting now."

Sam and her parents joined hands and came to the edge of the stage. The crowd went wild. Cameras flashed everywhere. In the midst of it all, Sam found Mia standing next to Ed—the guy of her dreams.

"Thank you," Mia mouthed, her face glowing.

Sam smiled back. And then her father cued the band. As Sam followed him to the dance floor, the reporter who had grilled her before the accident at the fund-raising gala appeared. "What do you think of your father's policies now, Samantha?"

"I've got my own policies to think about," she said, breezing past him. Her father extended his hand, she took it, and they started to dance.

"Funny thing about home," Sam mused. "It's not really about the house you live in on the outside, but how you live"—she touched his heart—"in here. Don't you think?"

"I do," he agreed.

"One thing you've taught me, Dad, is to make sure I'm always at home, no matter what anyone thinks," Sam told him. "And that has to include you." She was startled as her father stopped dancing to peer over her shoulder. She turned and . . . there he was. James stood before them, dressed in a tux.

Her father stepped aside and James walked up to her. "Place your left hand—"

"What are you—"

"Dancing with you," James explained, taking her hand. "Here. On my shoulder."

"We shouldn't," Sam protested feebly,

certain he could hear her heart pounding. "We can't."

"And try not to lead this time, okay?" He smiled down at her. "Trust me."

She did. They danced cheek to cheek as the band played on, whirling past Mia, who was in the middle of a long, slow dance with a smitten Ed. When the music came to an end, James reached into his suit pocket and removed a car key. "I believe this is yours. We did everything to your exact specifications."

"Thank you, James," Sam said, accepting the key.

They stood there, and Sam was pretty sure he didn't want the moment to end either. "Number of times I've watched the movie *In the Line of Fire*—twenty-seven," James said finally.

"Number of miles between Pennsylvania Avenue and Woody House—three thousand, three hundred and eighty-one." Sam gave a sheepish shrug. "Number of times I've calculated that: roughly the same."

At last, they couldn't stall any longer. James leaned in and kissed Sam on the forehead. "Bye, Sam. Now go try and break a few rules, okay?"

"And you try to keep some," she replied lightly, struggling to keep the emotion from her voice. She turned and walked slowly through the ball, past one dignitary after another, as if she were in a dream. A very bad dream.

Outside, she stopped on the steps, the cool night air a wake-up call to her brain cells. Press corps and politicians or not, this was no way to say goodbye. She turned and raced back inside—where she practically crashed into James, who was running at breakneck speed toward her.

"Forget something?" Sam asked breathlessly.

"Yeah." And he took her into his arms and kissed her as if he would never let her go.

"Wow," Sam said as they pulled apart. "I just forgot my purse." Then she lowered her voice. "Take good care of him."

"I will." He held up his watch. "I'm just getting back on duty now."

"And I'm just getting off." She squeezed his hand and watched as he headed back into the thick of things inside. Her father was standing not that far from her, and as she locked eyes with him, he gave her a subtle yet clear nod of approval.

With her head spinning and her heart full of emotion, she headed back outside once more, walking down the steps to find a battered old Volkswagen Beetle—just like the one she had described to Liz Pappas before she'd left for school. She ran toward it in her high heels, elated.

This is too cool! she thought as she climbed inside, tucking the folds of her ball gown underneath her. She put the key in the ignition, turned on the radio, and pulled away.

Leaving James was one of the hardest things she had to do.

But she'd be home for spring break in a few months.

And considering that James was part of her father's new security detail, she had a feeling she could hear about him whenever she wanted to.

As she came to a stoplight, she reached over to the passenger seat and opened the small cooler, just like the one she had wished for back in August. Inside were granola bars, fruit snacks, crackers, mini cheeses, and bologna sandwiches. She picked up a sandwich. Underneath was a can of soda. She scowled—then broke into laughter.

If all her wishes except this one had come true, life was looking pretty good.

The light turned green and Sam cruised down the street.

In fact, from where she sat on a time-softened leather bucket seat, life was looking fantastic.

About**the**Author

Christa Roberts lives in New Jersey and has never flown on Air Force One—but is available should the opportunity arise.